Praise for

FINDING BEAR

'A triumphant return to April and Bear's world, this time with the loveliest baby bear. A roaringly snowy adventure'
Nizrana Farook, author of *The Girl Who Stole an Elephant*

'An unstoppable, heartwarming sequel. I'll be recommending this book forever'
Carlie Sorosiak, author of *I, Cosmo*

'Revisiting the world of April and Bear feels like coming in from the cold. Magical'
Rob Biddulph, author of *Peanut Jones and the Illustrated City*

'Pack your rainbow boots for the most magnificent adventure! An exhilarating story of love, hope and courage'
Jenny Pearson, author of *The Super Miraculous Journey of Freddie Yates*

'Pure joy . . . An immensely powerful story'
Jasbinder Bilan, author of *Asha & the Spirit Bird*

'A cold story that makes you feel warm and fuzzy inside'
Lee Newbery, author of *The Last Firefox*

'A beautiful, breathtaking Arctic adventure. Made my heart pound, break and soar!'
Rashmi Sirdeshpande, author of *Never Show a T-Rex a Book*

Books by Hannah Gold

THE LAST BEAR

THE LOST WHALE

FINDING BEAR

FINDING BEAR

HANNAH GOLD

Illustrated by Levi Pinfold

HarperCollins *Children's Books*

First published in the United Kingdom by
HarperCollins *Children's Books* in 2023
HarperCollins *Children's Books* is a division of HarperCollins*Publishers* Ltd
1 London Bridge Street
London SE1 9GF

www.harpercollins.co.uk

HarperCollins*Publishers*
Macken House, 39/40 Mayor Street Upper
Dublin 1, D01 C9W8, Ireland

4

Text copyright © Hannah Gold 2023
Illustrations copyright © Levi Pinfold 2023
Cover design copyright © HarperCollins*Publishers* Ltd 2023
All rights reserved

HB ISBN 978-0-00-858201-2
Waterstones special edition HB ISBN 978-0-00-863967-9

Hannah Gold and Levi Pinfold assert the moral right to be identified as the author
and illustrator of the work respectively.

A CIP catalogue record for this title is available from the British Library.

Typeset in Aldus LT Std 12/21pt
Printed and bound in the UK using 100% renewable electricity at CPI Group (UK) Ltd

This book is produced from independently certified FSC™ paper
to ensure responsible forest management.

For more information visit: www.harpercollins.co.uk/green

To every single person who wanted April and Bear to reunite.

This book is for you.

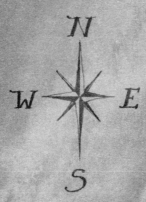

NORTH POLE
650 mi

SVALBARD

N

W E

S

BEAR ISLAND
238 mi

CHAPTER ONE

The Photograph

It was exactly seventeen months since April Wood had returned home from Bear Island and she was sitting cross-legged in her back garden listening to the sound of silence. Other people might have said that silence can't make a noise, but April knew differently.

She knew that silence carried all sorts of messages

– especially if you had learned how to listen properly. Besides, she much preferred being outdoors to inside. It was an altogether kinder place.

Particularly these days.

When April and her father had first arrived back from the Arctic, it had been like diving into the deep end of a very cold swimming pool. The constant noise and smog of cars and motorbikes, with their never-ending stench of exhaust, had been the most horrible shock. And *people.* So many people everywhere. Hustling, bustling and jostling every crowded minute of the day.

It had been Dad's decision to hasten the move to the seaside and within a month, they had sold their tall and gloomy city house and found somewhere new near Granny Apples. It wasn't necessarily the kind of house April would have chosen herself. Number Thirty-Four, Stirling Road sat in a row of identical modern red-brick houses, each with its own neatly lawned back garden and freshly painted fence. Unlike their old home, or even the wooden cabin on Bear Island, this house was filled with hard, square corners and shiny, gleaming work surfaces. There wasn't even an open fire to toast crumpets on. Instead, it had one of those electric fires with pretend logs that glowed red with the flick of a switch. But Dad seemed happy. In fact, he was the happiest April had seen him in years and, as he kept reminding her, this house was far easier to keep clean.

But it didn't mean she had to stay inside, especially on an evening like this – when the setting sun was streaking the sky with shades of gold and the breeze whispered through the trees like magic.

'It's beautiful,' she said out loud.

That was another thing that had remained with her from the Arctic. The habit of speaking out loud to herself. April didn't consider it strange. Not until others started giving her funny looks.

Thankfully it was a Friday, which meant school was over for the week and she could do exactly as she wanted. She'd only been there a handful of months but still hadn't shaken off the feeling of being the odd one out.

It didn't help that after her presentation about the plight of the polar bears – the one that had taken *ages* to prepare – most of the class had just yawned. When April had tried to wake them up with her best roar (one she was very proud of) and then demonstrated how she could smell peanut butter from over one mile away, all they'd done was laugh and then make bear noises at her from the back of the class. To make matters even more embarrassing, the teacher had pulled her aside and suggested that perhaps animal impersonations were best kept out of the classroom.

April had tried to explain in her best and most polite voice that it *wasn't* an impersonation. That she was trying to inform everyone about the problems in the Arctic – just like Lisé from the Polar Institute had encouraged her. But her words were wasted. From that moment on, she was known as 'Bear Girl' and, judging from the accompanying sniggers, she wasn't sure it was a compliment.

The article in the local press hadn't helped either.

Somehow a local reporter had got wind of April and her father's trip to the Arctic and since it was a slow news week, he'd wanted to tell their story. Dad had been reluctant. But not April. She had seized the opportunity because surely here was a chance to tell everyone about how much the polar bears needed their help. Here was a chance to warn people how quickly the Arctic was melting! But then the article had got lots of facts wrong, including April's own name. As if she were anything like an Alice! And worst of all, rather than saying that *she* had saved Bear, the article implied that the captain of the ship had done all the hard work.

April wasn't looking for brownie points or gold stars or even compliments. All she wanted was for someone to take her seriously. Especially now time was ticking for the planet.

'If I really *was* Bear Girl,' she muttered, 'then people would be listening! They would be making changes!'

A crow perched on the fence cawed in agreement.

April sighed. It was February and despite a handful

of brave daffodils, the air still carried a brisk chill. No doubt Dad would call her in soon – worried she would catch hypothermia or some other life-threatening condition. Ever since they had got back from the Arctic, he constantly worried about her and fretted non-stop that she would fall into some terrible danger. Even now she could see him through the kitchen window searching for her, which meant she only had minutes left.

She carefully took a photograph out of her pocket. It was the safest place for it, but more importantly, it also meant it was pressed to her heart at all times. It wasn't the kind of photo most people carried in their pockets. It wasn't a photo of a mum or a dad or brothers and sisters or grandmas and grandpas. This was a photo of her and a full-sized male polar bear – huddled together in a tight embrace that would seem incredulous to most people. It was, of course, a photo of her and Bear and it was her most treasured possession. Taken on the quayside in Longyearbyen, Svalbard, the pair of them were silhouetted against the sun, leaning into

one another as the flash of the camera caught their final goodbyes. They were pressed so tightly together that it was hard to see where Bear ended and girl began. Even now, April couldn't look at the photo without feeling a horrible tightness in her throat.

'Hello, Bear,' she whispered, hearing the tremble in her voice.

April wasn't sure how long polar bear memories lasted, or even if Bear remembered her at all. Not in the same way she remembered him, anyway. She would never ever forget him. Not for as long as she lived. And then for a trillion more years on top of that.

No doubt he was getting on with his new life. The way that Dad said she ought to be getting on with hers. It wasn't like she hadn't *tried*. Every day she did her best to live the kind of life that Dad, Granny Apples and everyone else seemed to expect from her – a perfectly normal human existence. And that might have been enough for some people. But every so often, a memory would surface in April's mind – the tickly sensation of Bear's whiskers on her face, the sudden touch of his wet nose and, most vivid of all, the warm soft chocolate of his eyes and the way his gaze had melted into her own.

'I miss you,' she said quietly, making sure Dad couldn't hear through the open kitchen window. 'I miss you *so* much.'

She didn't expect a reply. The Arctic, after all, was a long way away and April hadn't heard from Bear since their last fateful day together. Bear couldn't write letters or pick up the phone and it was much too far away to hear him roar. But he had, hopefully, found some new polar bear friends – maybe even a mate. Most of all, she hoped he was happy.

'Because that was the whole point of taking you back to Svalbard, wasn't it?' she whispered. 'I just wish . . . I wish I knew that you were all right.'

April breathed in the silence, hoping that somewhere out in the night sky she might receive the answer she longed for. As she strained her ears, she heard the whisper of the silver birch tree, the bark of a dog two streets down, the distant tremor of the sea. But what she couldn't hear was . . .

'APRIL!' Dad flung open the back door and a puddle of warm yellow light spilled out. 'What are you doing out here? You'll catch your death of cold!'

'I'm coming,' she said, reluctantly standing, the evening peace suddenly shattered. She slipped the photo back into her breast pocket and zipped it up tight. Then, as the crow continued to caw, she followed her father inside.

Chapter Two

Rainbow Wellies

April wiped her feet carefully on the mat before placing her shoes in the cupboard. As she did, she caught a flash of something bright and colourful hiding at the back. Her rainbow wellies. They were too small for her now and even though she probably should have taken them to a charity shop long ago, she hadn't. It was one of the few links she had left to Bear Island, and if she put her nose closely to them, she could have sworn she could smell the faint sharp air of the Arctic. She was half tempted to smell them now but her father called her again.

She entered the living room to find the floor covered in a carpet of vinyl. 'I was trying to find . . . ah! Here it is.' He plucked out the record triumphantly. 'Did you have a good day?'

'It was fine,' she answered, crossing her fingers behind her back.

'Good, good,' Dad said, smiling at her lopsidedly. 'That's my girl. I knew you'd be happy here.'

April winced. Now in her third term at her new school, she didn't have the heart to tell him that she'd struggled to make any real friends yet. For some mysterious reason, making friends with humans was far harder than it was with polar bears.

'How was your day?' she asked instead.

Just as he had promised, Dad had taken on a job at

the local university trying to come up with compostable alternatives for single-use plastic. He was about to answer when the doorbell clanged.

'Ah!' he said, flushing. 'That'll be Maria. I asked her over for dinner. I . . . I hope you don't mind? I know normally it's just us . . . '

He was looking at her so earnestly that April nodded. Although she never would have admitted it out loud, she was a teeny bit disappointed. Friday night was *their* night. The one evening where Dad finished work early so they could have some 'together' time. Tonight, she'd hoped they could try out that new vegan restaurant in town, or even take a walk along the beach. Just the two of them.

Dad paused in front of the hallway mirror, brushed a hand through his dishevelled hair and adjusted his collar before opening the door.

'Maria!' he exclaimed. 'You look . . . well! And you brought Chester with you. Good, good. April loves Chester, don't you?!'

Without question, April loved Chester. Who wouldn't? He was a cockerpoo with honey-coloured eyes, soft velvety ears and a delicious doggy smell that she found irresistible.

'Edmund!' Maria entered the hallway in a blaze of colour and a waft of saffron. 'I've brought paella for the dinner.'

Maria often brought food. She was from Valencia in Spain and loved to cook for people. Either that or she was fed up with Dad's cooking. Neither April nor her father had lost the habit of eating their food out of tin cans, much to Granny Apples's disgust, who said that some habits should stay in the Arctic where they belonged.

Dad and Maria did that awkward grown-up thing of hugging but not really hugging before letting their hands flap uselessly by their sides. Both of them wore silly grins that said far more than words ever could. It was then Maria noticed April.

'Hello there!' she said, taking off her red-dotted scarf and smiling widely.

April nodded back. It wasn't that she didn't *like* Maria. After all, hadn't she wanted Dad to get a girlfriend? Plus, she wasn't the kind of person to truly dislike anyone – especially not someone who loved animals. It was just, well, a teeny bit awkward when your headteacher was also your dad's new girlfriend. This was how Dad had met her – at the gates of April's new school. April was never quite sure whether to call her Miss Puro or Maria, so half the time she ended up avoiding calling her anything at all.

As always, Chester helped smooth over any embarrassing silences. He scampered across to April with a hopeful expression. 'Hello, boy,' she whispered as Maria trailed after Dad into the living room.

'I found this piece of music earlier that I wanted to play for you,' Dad uttered, waving one of his records in the air like it was some sort of trophy. 'I think you're going to love it.'

He placed it on the record player, the same one that had been to the Arctic and back, and within seconds, the sound of Mozart's *Voi Che Sapete* from 'The Marriage of Figaro' filled the air. It was an upbeat, almost jaunty song. Composed for laughter, sunshiny days and skipping.

Dad, who was by no means a natural dancer, had been taking lessons and he encircled Maria in his arms and began to vigorously twirl her around the room in a waltz. The paella dish lay forgotten on the floor and April stood in the doorway, looking in, with an uncomfortable ache in her chest. An ache she didn't quite understand but one that made her feel guilty for feeling it at all.

'What is it, my dear girl?' Dad asked over dinner, the three of them sitting around the paella dish at the kitchen table. 'Something seems to be bothering you.'

Once upon a time, her father would never have noticed her moods – not even if April had skipped and cartwheeled her way into a room singing at the top of her voice.

Whilst he still wasn't the most observant person in the universe, Dad had nevertheless changed. And even though she had wanted this change – including a new girlfriend for him – when it had come it was so fast and so sudden, it had caught her off-guard. The feeling was unsettling. As though Dad's life had galloped gamely on whereas her feet were stuck somewhere in the thick, unremitting ice of the Arctic.

Dad didn't even like to talk about their experiences

much. Oh, he showed photographs to some of his work colleagues and she'd once overheard him boasting about how living in the Arctic changed a human from the inside out. But when it actually came to talking about their time on Bear Island – *the adventure the two of them had shared together* – he was strangely mute. April put it down to the fact he had almost lost her. That and his guilt at initially not believing her about her friendship with Bear.

All of which made it quite difficult for her to admit to missing the Arctic – especially in front of Maria who, as far as April was aware, only knew the sketchiest version of what had really happened. And even if she *did* feel comfortable talking about it, then she'd have to find the right words and that simply was not possible. How could April ever explain how much she missed Bear? It was not just a feeling in her heart – but something much rawer that seemed to echo within the deepest parts of her.

It was word*less.*

It was as if she had left part of her behind when she left the Arctic. Not a mitten, or a wellie or anything tangible. But the part which made her April. Like the sound of her laughter as it echoed across the island, or the grin on her face as she clutched on to Bear's fur as they clambered up the mountain, or the bottomless feeling in her heart as she gazed into Bear's eyes and he gazed back.

April realised her father was still looking at her and expecting an answer. 'Nothing's wrong,' she answered. If Maria hadn't been there, he might have pressed it, but as it was, he got distracted and so the moment passed.

After eating, the three of them settled down to a game of Monopoly. Maria chose the dog, April picked the boat, whilst Dad insisted on using an aniseed candy as his marker – which he ended up eating halfway through.

Very soon April had lost all her money. Not that she particularly cared. When she was grown up and had lots of money, she'd do more with it than buy silly houses. She'd put it towards something which made a difference. Something which wasn't just bricks and mortar. Something *important*.

Anyway, it was nearly time for bed. And the sooner she could go to bed, the sooner she could wake up.

Because tomorrow was the day when Tör's next email would arrive.

She'd only met Tör twice in her life – once on the boat on the way to Bear Island and then again after he'd helped rescue her from the icy sea. Nevertheless, he was still her truest friend. The one human who seemed to perfectly understand her. That was the thing with shared experiences – they blended you together in ways that lasted forever.

Although April read lots of articles on the internet and watched documentaries about the Arctic, it wasn't the same as actually being there. Which made Tör's emails all the more special. After his ship had made its monthly docking in Svalbard, he would wander around the settlement, taking photos, even the occasional video (one time of a reindeer wandering down Longyearbyen's main street!), but mostly collecting the latest news and then reporting it back to April – including any up-to-date information from the Polar Institute. Once in a while Lisé also sent a message, although these days she seemed to be busy on various field trips, and so April was mainly reliant on Tör to be her eyes and ears.

Being such a remote archipelago of islands where no food could grow – indeed there weren't even any trees on Svalbard – the inhabitants depended on the outside world for almost everything. Tör's ship was due to arrive tomorrow morning, and as the son of a ship's captain, timetables and punctuality were ingrained on his soul.

He had never, ever, been late with an email.

As April said goodnight to her father and Maria, she felt a quickening in her heart. A skippy light feeling – as if the record player was still playing music but now only *she* could hear it. It was the same every month. Tör's emails weren't just words on a screen. They were living, breathing things that brought with them the scent of the Arctic and precious glimpses of a world that still beckoned her with its icy fingertips.

In truth, it was the only time of the month that April felt truly alive.

CHAPTER THREE

The Email

Perhaps it was the warmth which gave April the bad dream.

Her father always turned the heating up when Maria came over as she often complained about their house being chilly. It was true that neither April nor her father ever put the heating on particularly high. Partly for environmental reasons, but mostly because the Arctic blood still flowed through their veins, whether Dad liked it or not. And even though Maria had long gone home, the heat smothered the house like a blanket.

She was back in the Arctic. But not with Bear. He was nowhere to be seen. This time she was alone. Single-handedly climbing up the side of the steepest of mountains with the sea pounding at her feet and the frosty wind blowing in her ears. When she finally reached the summit, she gazed around frantically.

'*Bear*?' she called, hating the way her voice quavered. 'BEAR*?!*'

Nothing answered except the grey clouds billowing angrily overhead. Then she spotted it. A tuft of soft white fur trapped under a rock. She knelt down, and with a racing heart, she pulled it free, pressing the fur to her nose. It smelled of something musky, feral and alive. But it also smelled of home.

With a start, April realised that she was facing north. And that many months ago she had been sitting in this exact same spot, gazing out over the harsh, steely sea and listening to Bear's story.

'Bear?' she asked again.

She cocked her head and listened across time and space until there, on the furthest edges of the world, she heard a noise. A noise she would have recognised anywhere.

It was Bear's roar.

ROARING.

Roaring.

Roaring.

The roar felt so real and so raw that it woke April up.

At first, she was confused, imagining she was still on the tip of the mountain with the lick of Arctic air on her lips. Then the bedroom gradually took shape. The outline of her wardrobe, her sturdy wooden writer's bureau and finally, the glint of all the photos on the wall shining back the iridescent landscape of the far north.

Outside the window a car engine vroomed loudly and, despite the lateness of the hour, April sat bolt upright in bed. Because there in the far distance, far beyond her house, her street, her country – far beyond any distance any human ought to be able to hear – she could have sworn she heard something else.

The unmistakable sound of a roar.

As the next morning passed in a never-ending haze of tasks and errands and dull, grown-up things to do, April began to question herself. Had she *really* heard Bear roar last night? Or was it just a dream? A wishful figment of her imagination?

It had sounded so real. And it was precisely that realness which left her with a strange, uneasy sensation in the pit of her belly, one that wouldn't go away no matter how hard she tried to shake it. At least today she would hear from Tör. He usually sent his email before lunch, once the crew had unloaded their cargo. Just the thought of it sent a shimmer of excitement through her.

If only Dad would hurry up! On the way back from the garage, he had decided to stop at the sweet shop to stock up on aniseed candy. The shop was located in the town centre. Any other day, April would have loved to go shopping with him – not to buy stuff she didn't need, but to look in the charity shops to see if they had any polar bear ornaments. But today, she opted to wait in the car, trying her hardest not to keep checking her watch.

'C'mon, Dad!' she muttered. He had been at least five whole minutes already.

As she fidgeted in her seat, she caught sight of two girls from her class at school, walking arm in arm down the street. The taller girl – the one with blonde pigtails and pink ribbons – had been the first to call her Bear Girl. She'd once even said April smelled like an animal.

April didn't consider this an insult. Everyone knew that animals smelled of magic. But nevertheless, she ducked low until the pair of them had passed. If there was one thing she had learned in the past seventeen months, it was to avoid wasting time on people who didn't see you for who you truly were.

Finally, Dad appeared, carrying the sweets in his

hands like they were gold bullion. 'Sorry about the delay,' he said, clumsily manoeuvring his long limbs into the car. 'Bit of a queue.'

She willed him to start the engine and get going. Because surely by now, Tör's email would be here? It would be waiting for her!

'I thought we could pop in and see Granny Apples on our way home?' he suggested, unwrapping a sweet and popping it into his mouth with a contented sigh.

'NO!!' April exclaimed, then softened her voice at the sight of Dad's alarmed face. 'Another day maybe.'

Dad nodded, his eyebrows creasing together in befuddlement before starting the car. 'Home time it is!'

As soon as she was through the door, April kicked off her shoes so they landed with a clatter on the hallway floor. Then she raced up the stairs, not caring that she hadn't taken off her coat and it was flapping around her heels. Not even bothering to take each step – but throwing herself at them two, three at a time. Until she launched herself into her bedroom, flung open the laptop and opened her inbox.

Her chest rose and fell in noisy rasps and it took a few seconds before she could focus on the screen properly.

And when she did . . .

How strange.

There were no new emails.

Nothing.

April had three timepieces. A wall clock which showed the local time. Another clock that showed the time in Svalbard and the watch Dad had given her on her first day on Bear Island. She checked all three of them to be certain. (She also had a fourth one which showed how long it would take for the planet to heat up beyond repair. But she kept that one in her desk drawer as it was the kind of thing which didn't do you much good to stare at all the time.)

Having checked the internet was definitely on, she rebooted her computer just to make sure it was working properly. But still no email appeared. April mentally ran through various scenarios.

• Tor's ship could have docked late. The weather in the Arctic was very temperamental, after all.

• He might have been busy on an errand for his father.

• He was busy writing an extra-juicy email with lots of photos which was so data heavy, it was taking a long time to upload. (Although this was unlikely as Tör's emails tended to be quite short and lacking the colour April would have sometimes preferred. She supposed it was a boy thing.)

But, as she glanced at the picture of her and Bear again, somewhere in the pit of her tummy the uneasy feeling grew and grew. And out of the window the crow cawed in agreement.

It wasn't until after dinner that Tör's email arrived.

April had been dozing. Not a nice, gentle, relaxing doze. But a restless one. The kind where your mind chops and churns. The ping of the incoming email was like the clanging of a ship's horn, jolting her awake.

As she reached down to pick the laptop up, time

slowed. As if all three clocks in the room had paused momentarily and were holding their breath. Part of her wanted to grab the laptop, whilst the other half wanted to pull the duvet over her face. But April was not someone who hid from things. Not even if they brought the worst of news. Instead, she took a steadying breath and opened the email.

A polar bear has been shot in Longyearbyen.
I think it's Bear.

Chapter Four

No Time To Lose

Dad had been watching a documentary on grey whales, but one look at April's face and he jumped to his feet and turned the television off. Over a pot of hot chocolate and an emergency jar of marshmallows, he prised the story out of her.

'But April, how can Tör be certain about this? There

are countless polar bears on Svalbard.'

'Around three thousand,' April replied, taking a shaky sip of her drink.

When she had first read the email, it was as if she herself had been shot. A sensation so sharp and piercing it had ripped her breath clean away. She'd ended up gulping for air. Short, frantic, horrible gasps. But however hard she gulped, the pain just kept getting sharper.

Even with the comforting arm of her father around her shoulders, she still felt as though she were underwater, frantically trying to find her way to the surface. But this time there was no Bear to rescue her.

'But, my dear child,' Dad's voice softened, 'out of those three thousand polar bears, how can Tör possibly think that this is *your* bear?'

April flinched. 'Not just my bear,' she replied. '*Bear*. His name is Bear. And yes, he does know because . . . because . . . '

She couldn't finish the sentence. Not without wanting

to scream or clench her fists into tight bunches. Instead, she pointed out the attachment.

SVALBARD NEWS
POLAR BEAR SHOT IN LONGYEARBYEN

On Friday evening, a male polar bear was shot and wounded in Longyearbyen port by person unknown but presumed to be a tourist.

Eyewitnesses said that the bear had been spotted in the port on three consecutive nights, with one saying: 'He was in the same position every night, standing on his two feet, staring out to sea and roaring.'

In the past few years, climate change has damaged polar bears' habitat, often forcing them to scavenge for food on land and, increasingly, come into contact with humans. Scientists warn of their increasingly volatile behaviour as the sea ice continues to melt and advise against humans getting too close to them.

Polar bears are listed as endangered animals and whilst it is a legal requirement to carry a firearm in Svalbard, it is strongly advised only to shoot a bear if your life is in immediate danger.

It is not known what happened to the bear.

Her father read the article twice. Then he slowly took off his glasses, rubbed his eyes and stared unseeingly at his daughter.

'Don't you get it?!' April cried, thinking not just of the article but of her unsettling dream. 'It *has* to be Bear. Which other bear would come to the exact place in that port and rear up on its hind legs like that?'

'But why would he come back?'

It was a good question. Because surely, Bear must have

known, as all wild animals know on some deep instinctive level, that being in town and around humans could only mean danger. So why had he put himself at such risk?

The answer struck her like a flash of lightning. He had come because he needed her! She didn't know why, but she knew, in the very fibre of her being, that Bear was calling for her.

'He needs me,' she said. 'He needs me and now he's got hurt.'

Maybe even . . .

Somewhere beneath April, the Earth tilted violently and it was all she could do to cling on. No. She couldn't think *that*. Instead, she leaned forward, planted her elbows firmly on the table and looked her father square in the eye. 'We have to help him.'

'Help him? But what can we do from here?'

'Not much,' she admitted. 'That's why we need to go back.'

'Go back to *Svalbard*?' Dad swallowed. 'No! Absolutely No Way!'

He took a long slurp of his hot chocolate and when he put the mug down, he had a moustache of milk on his upper lip. Normally, April would have wiped it away or at least pointed it out. But his face was so pensive, this time she did neither.

'Look,' he said, jabbing the article. 'It says "it is not known what happened to the bear". The truth is the . . . *Bear* might be fine. We could make all this effort and he could be perfectly unharmed.'

'But what if he isn't?' April said quietly. 'What if he's injured?'

'I would question what we would be able to do about it.'

'Oh, Dad,' April sighed. She placed a hand over his. Under her touch, she felt him tremble. She squeezed his hand gently in response. 'I can't just leave him . . . you know I can't. I wouldn't be able to live with myself. I . . . I wouldn't be able to live *at all*. Even if he isn't injured, I need to find out why he was calling me.' Her mind turned once again to the dream and how she had heard Bear's roar when she woke up. 'There's something wrong. I just know it.'

Dad exhaled slowly and placed his hands palm down on the table. He had a firm look in his eye she didn't like. It was the kind of look that suggested a no was coming, so she spoke quickly to intercept it.

'Once upon a time I told you something very important and you didn't believe me,' she said. 'Then I did something very dangerous but only because I didn't know what else to do. And in the process . . . ' Her voice tailed off. Even now, April found it difficult to think about the moment she'd fallen in the ice-cold sea and nearly drowned.

'And in the process,' Dad answered falteringly, finishing the sentence for her, 'I . . . I almost lost you.'

April nodded, hardly daring to say any more but knowing she had to push. 'After that you said you would do everything in your power to make it up to me. You *promised*.'

Dad let out a long shuddering sigh. One that April wasn't sure how to interpret. But she kept her hand on his. As if he were a ship that needed steadying. His face contorted into a thousand different shapes before he settled on an expression of deep resignation.

'I did promise and . . . and I still mean it,' he said in a voice that shook ever so slightly at the edges.

'Then *please*, Dad?' April said. 'Please will you take me back?'

There was no time to lose. Unlike previously, there was no opportunity to go to a specialist shop to pick out winter clothes, so this time they simply grabbed what they had from the wardrobe. Given that he never truly expected to return any time soon, Dad had long since donated most of his Arctic attire to charity shops. The only things he had left were a pair of woollen base layers, a waterproof jacket plus a very long mustard yellow scarf Maria had knitted for him for Christmas. April fared little better. Even though she had kept all her clothing, she had outgrown most of it. Nevertheless, a thick winter jacket, a bobble hat and various warm layers were better than nothing. The only thing neither of them had were proper snow boots.

'There are bound to be shops out there selling the right sort of equipment,' Dad said.

'I hope so. It will be minus-ten degrees and goodness me, that's just in the daytime!' Maria said, pulling a horrified face.

Dad had insisted on calling Maria as soon as they

had made their decision, and despite the lateness of the hour, she had been at their house within minutes. April wasn't sure how Maria would react. It was all so last-minute and there were no guarantees as to how long they would be gone.

But April had been surprised.

Even though Maria had no real sense of their mission, she seemed to understand intuitively how important the trip was to April. It was Maria who had the foresight to book them into a hotel – luckily, despite the late notice, she'd managed to find one with a family room. And it was Maria who was calm enough to reserve the air travel.

'I've managed to get two seats on a flight which leaves midday tomorrow.'

April felt bad about flying. It was, after all, one of the major causes of climate change. But faced with a choice of boarding a boat and it taking over a week to get there, or arriving tomorrow, she knew there was no alternative. Instead, she vowed to donate a whole month's worth of pocket money to a company that planted trees to offset carbon emissions. Not perfect. But better than nothing. And sometimes doing the best you can is good enough.

Luckily Dad had some leave owing to him at work and Maria said she would smooth things out at April's school. The only obstacle that now stood in their way wore pink slippers and smelled of apples.

'I can't believe you're taking her back, Edmund! Not after last time!'

It was the morning of their flight and with the bags packed, it was far too late for protests.

Outside the house, a taxi hooted its horn. Dad pulled Maria into a tight embrace, closing his eyes and brushing his lips against her hair. It was such an intimate, personal moment that April felt guilty for witnessing it at all.

'Come here,' spluttered Granny Apples, yanking her into a fierce goodbye hug before letting her go with a loud sniff. 'Take care of yourself this time. You promise me that.'

April gave her grandmother an extra-big squeeze

in response. As the taxi tooted its horn once more, Dad gave one last goodbye kiss to Maria.

'It's time,' he said, clearing his throat.

Chester barked with excitement. There was just one final thing to do. April plucked a jar of peanut butter from the kitchen cupboard and popped it in her suitcase.

'I'm ready,' she said.

CHAPTER FIVE

Return to Svalbard

APRIL HAD ONLY ever seen the Arctic from the bow of the ship or from the back of a polar bear. Granted, these were interesting perspectives. But still very different compared to seeing it from the window of a plane thousands of metres up in the sky.

This was their third and final flight. The first one had

taken them to Oslo, the capital of Norway. They had then flown north to Tromsø – where all those months ago Dad and April had first set sail to Bear Island on Tör's cargo ship. This time their stay in Tromsø was far shorter – in fact the plane only stopped to refuel before jetting off again, headed directly to Longyearbyen.

April kept her eyes glued to the window. Since October, the Arctic had lain still and hushed under the weight of a long winter. This was the polar night, where darkness reigned over everything. But now, in mid-February, the sun was starting its return journey and the sky was a mysterious blue-black – a permanent twilight spreading out as far as April could see. Somewhere far below was Bear Island. A tiny speck in the ocean. But also, the place of her greatest adventure. Little things, big power.

But this time the destination wasn't Bear Island.

The plane flew for just over an hour before finally descending through a bank of dense cloud. As it did, April gasped.

Far below her was a white carpet of snow and ice coating the ground, so endless, it was hard to see where the land ended and the sea ice began. Even in the semi-darkness, the white shone so bright that it made her eyes smart.

Dad didn't gasp. In fact he didn't even look out of the window. He hadn't spoken much on the journey, except to complain he had forgotten to bring his bag of aniseed candy or to moan about how uncomfortable the seat was, or to remind April that she was NOT under ANY circumstances to put herself in danger whilst looking for Bear.

April nodded. It was easier to agree.

The plane was only partially full – Svalbard in winter was not top of most people's destinations. Those who were on board were grizzled, weather-beaten folk, who bore faces that looked as if they had gone to the edge of the earth and back again. There was also a group of excitable university students, no doubt headed out for scientific research. And then finally a smattering of tourists, drawn by the lure of adventure and the siren call of the Arctic.

April was the youngest person on the plane.

She touched her fingertips against the window, feeling the chill press back. Last time April and her father had travelled to the Arctic Circle, it had been summertime. It might not have been warm, but there had been weeks and weeks of endless sunshine and countless days unpunctured by the dark of night.

But now? It would be achingly cold. Much colder than Bear Island since Svalbard sat further north and was even closer to the North Pole – the northernmost point of the whole planet. The archipelago of islands would be covered with snow, ice and glaciers. As the plane banked, April consulted her diary where, over the past year and a half, she had made countless notes about the Arctic plus the occasional doodle of a polar bear. She turned to the page where she'd written about winter conditions and took a sharp intake of breath. Temperatures could drop as low as minus-thirty at night. There would be howling winds, unpredictable storms, thick snow flurries, freezing fog and, of course, there would be polar bears. Bears that could kill.

The Arctic in winter was not a place you went to lightly.

The captain announced that they were beginning their descent and April gripped Dad's hand. After a short pause, he squeezed in return.

'We're back,' she whispered.

In the distance were a few bright yellow lights. Longyearbyen – a small town carved out of the wilderness with a main street, a row of shops, a handful of hotels and even a school. A place of only a couple of thousand inhabitants who came from all corners of the globe to live, work, study and protect the environment.

The plane banked and then sank lower, low enough for April to make out the individual wooden cabins lit up by the warm flickering lights within. So close she could see the outline of the port, where all those months ago she had sailed away and said goodbye to part of her heart.

Then suddenly the plane was gliding over the runway like one of those strange Arctic gulls that skimmed across the surface of the water, before silently touching down and eventually coming to a gentle rest.

April let out an involuntary sigh. A sigh she didn't even know she was holding, but which had been stuck in the deepest part of her for over a year. One which only emerged now they were back in the Arctic Circle. And despite the circumstances that had brought her here, April couldn't help but smile.

She was home.

Chapter Six

Hamish and Jurgen

It wasn't until the plane doors opened and the gush of achingly cold air coiled its way into the cabin, that April truly appreciated they were back. The air wasn't just cold. It was a dry, bitter cold. A cold that makes your eyes water, your skin thirsty and your lungs sting. She immediately pulled on her thick jacket and slipped on her bobble hat.

Dad's nose was already turning red and he blew it with a loud honk. 'We must find a place to buy some proper winter clothes, April. It would do us no good to freeze to death,' he muttered, briskly rubbing his hands together.

It didn't take long to pass through customs, after which they boarded a shuttle bus that picked up all passengers and took them directly to their respective hotels. Dad was insistent on this point. It had taken them the best part of the day to get here and he needed a hot cup of coffee and a rest before they were to do anything.

'April, my dear child,' he said reassuringly as if sensing her impatience. 'We must always make time for a plan . . . especially in this part of the world.'

Despite the impatient knots in her tummy, April knew he was right. Looming over the town were the sharp-toothed outlines of mountains, dark and forbidding silhouettes against a crescent moon. There was snow everywhere – piled high in uneven drifts against the buildings, layered thickly over rooftops and shovelled up in huge banks by the roadside. It was a new world. A harsh world. And most of all, a dangerous world.

Given there were only a handful of places to stay in town, the bus journey wasn't long. But whilst all the other passengers were dropped off at a smart-looking hotel in the main street, their own hotel sat at the top of a very steep hill.

At first glance, it didn't look like much. An ugly trio of interlinked cargo containers all on one level, set against the backdrop of the jagged mountain lurking above them.

Inside wasn't much better.

They were greeted by a dimly lit foyer and a large wooden reception desk covered in a faint coating of dust. April sniffed the air. The place smelled unused and had a forlorn, unhappy feel about it. On the wall behind the desk were black and white photographs of Longyearbyen depicting the history of the town from the early hunting expeditions to the later mining settlements, through to the more tourist-led community it was today. One of them made April curl her nose up in dismay. A gruesome photo of arctic fox skins hanging up in a row. She recoiled in disgust, swivelled round and came face to face with a  full-sized reindeer head stuck on the wall behind her. Its magnificent antlers were offset by dull brown eyes and a sad smile.

'Oh,' she murmured, 'you poor thing.'

She knew in the olden days people had come to Svalbard to hunt the wildlife for its meat and fur. But seeing it with her own eyes was something completely different. How had he ended up here? Stuck on some hotel wall? For such a noble animal, it was completely unfair.

'Ah! I see you've met Hamish!'

'Hamish?' April whirled round to see a slightly rotund gentleman, wearing a paisley waistcoat and deerstalker hat.

'The reindeer,' the man replied, chuckling a tad too loudly. 'Don't worry, he won't bite!'

April was about to retort when she felt Dad's gentle hand on her shoulder. 'Edmund Wood and my daughter, April,' he said, holding out his hand. 'We booked in yesterday.'

'Jurgen King,' the man replied. Behind him was an open door that led into a lounge. April presumed it was his own living area given there was a large sign on the door saying 'Private'. Hanging off Jurgen's waistcoat was an old-fashioned timepiece on a gold chain, which he inspected with a flourish. 'Good, good. You're early.'

Jurgen nodded approvingly, then consulted a handwritten ledger on the desk, which as far as April could see was perfectly empty of names except for theirs. Nevertheless, he made an elaborate show of running his finger down the page. 'Here you are.'

As he passed over the paperwork for Dad to sign, Jurgen turned a curious gaze to April as if he wasn't used to seeing children out here.

'Your first time?'

'Our second,' she said.

'The first time was somewhat of an accident,' Dad explained. 'This time is more of an . . . '

'Expedition,' April finished. 'To find a friend. A *good* friend.'

She wasn't going to explain to Jurgen that the good friend happened to be rather large, fond of peanut butter and covered in white fur.

'Ah, then the Arctic must have caught your heart. Not many come once. Even fewer return – especially at this time of year,' he said with a raised eyebrow. 'Anyway, follow me.'

He led the way down a gloomy corridor, past a number of closed doors. Without prompting, he explained how he had been born in Germany and brought his family over to Svalbard ten years ago before his wife and young daughter had returned home. 'My daughter loved it here but unfortunately my wife rather less so. The Arctic is not the most forgiving of places.' He stopped at a door at the very end of the corridor. 'I hope this will suit you both.'

It was a small, sparsely furnished room with worn wooden bunkbeds, a lightshade made of driftwood and an oblong-shaped window which looked out on to the dark mountain beyond.

After Jurgen had bid them goodnight, Dad flopped down on to the lower bunk, curled up on his side and let out a long, weary sigh. 'I had forgotten how lonely it was here. What makes a person choose to live somewhere so remote?'

April didn't answer. She wanted to say it was a yearning somewhere deep inside the soul, but she wasn't sure Dad would understand. Instead, she pressed her nose to the window.

'I know you want to get out there and start searching.' Dad's voice softened. 'But we must rest and build up our energy. Try to sleep, April.'

She nodded reluctantly. But long after her father had dropped off, and she had showered and climbed up to the top bunk, she found herself still wide awake. April tossed and turned this way and that, and finally sat up with a sigh.

'*Bear?*' she whispered. 'Are you out there?'

She pressed her nose to the window once more, hoping against hope to see the silhouette of a polar bear on the horizon, just like she had on the very first night she arrived on Bear Island. But as the thick winter's night settled in, this time she could see nothing but her own anxious reflection.

CHAPTER SEVEN

The Port

APRIL MUST HAVE dozed off at some point because she woke squished up at the very end of the top bunk, with one arm slung loosely over the covers. At first, she was confused. *What time was it?* Unlike back home, there was no grey light seeping through the crack in the curtains. No indication of dawn. Instead, the room remained dark and impenetrable, the sole noise the deep rhythmic breathing of her father and the occasional surprised snore.

It was only her watch that confirmed it was morning.

'Dad!' she said, leaping down from her bunk and shaking his shoulder. 'DAD! It's time to get up!'

In the breakfast area, Jurgen was nowhere to be seen, but there was a pot of lukewarm coffee on one of the tables and two bread rolls which were a bit stale. Luckily April didn't have much of an appetite, although Dad made a game effort of eating both.

'Pity there's no marmalade,' he said, wiping some stray crumbs from his chin.

April spread the map of Longyearbyen across the table. She'd picked it up at the airport before taking the shuttle bus. 'We're here,' she said, pointing at their hotel which sat on the outskirts of town. 'So I suggest the first place we check is the port and see if we can find any eyewitnesses to . . . what happened.'

'Makes sense.'

'I think we should go to the Polar Institute too,' April added. 'I emailed Lisé last night to let her know we were coming but I've not heard anything yet. If anyone knows if it really was Bear, then it'll be her.'

'And Tör?' Dad asked. 'With his local knowledge, he would be useful.'

'I've messaged him,' April said. 'But I'm not sure it would have got through in time. He might already have left on the boat back to the mainland.'

Dad nodded and then folded the map into small, meticulously neat squares. He cleared his throat twice before lowering his voice. 'You must be prepared, April.'

April hated lowered voices from grown-ups. It always seemed to mean bad news. She folded her arms protectively across her chest. 'Prepared for *what*?'

Dad took a long sip of coffee. 'There is a good chance . . . a good chance that *if* indeed it was the b . . . Bear and he did unfortunately get shot . . . ' The words stuttered to a stop and he cleared his throat again. 'Then he might not have survived.'

April swallowed down the thick knot in her throat and stared across the lounge, waiting for her breath to settle, before answering. 'But there is also a good chance he has,' she said, at last finding her voice. 'And I suggest we get looking.'

From their vantage point on top of the hill they could see the town laid out below them – a series of dotted lights and the flicker of water in the distance. The sun wasn't due to rise until eleven o'clock and the skies were a deep blue.

'Right,' Dad said, rubbing his hands together, 'I suggest before we go anywhere, we find some warm, appropriate clothes. I found a flier in the foyer and apparently there is an expedition shop on the main street.'

April knew this was the sensible thing to do. But the harbour was literally just *there*. And Dad always took such a long time choosing his shoes because his left foot was bigger than the right, and then invariably he would start chatting to the shop assistant and no doubt tell them how he liked his shoelaces tied exactly so because he was superstitious about things like that. And every minute that ticked by was a minute lost. Another minute wondering where Bear was and if he was all right.

No! She couldn't wait. Not now she was here. She just *couldn't*.

'Dad! Please can we go after we've been to the port?'

He glanced down at his footwear and then back at April's face. He sighed heavily. 'I suppose another few minutes won't hurt. Port first it is.'

It only took a handful of steps before April realised it might not have been the wisest decision. The terrain was a mixture of compacted snow and slick, invisible ice. At times, she couldn't even make out if they were walking on the pavement or the road as it had all blended into one continuous track. As they descended the hill, once or twice she lost her footing – sliding treacherously before her father reached out and pulled her upright. He fared only marginally better and kept Maria's scarf tightly wrapped around his neck for warmth.

Along the way the only other people they passed were a couple, holding hands. They were dressed in buttoned-down, ankle-length coats, fleece-lined boots and swathed in hats and scarves with mini skis attached to their feet.

April snuck her hand inside her dad's and felt comforted when he squeezed back. Neither spoke again until she ground to a halt, the smell of oil and brine and sea salt suddenly filling her nostrils and the sound of the angry, crashing waves bringing back memories she had tried very hard to forget.

'Well, here we are,' Dad said quietly.

It had been seventeen months since she'd last set foot on Longyearbyen port, and yet, in the way that time was a mysterious, unquantifiable thing, it also felt like yesterday.

There was the quay where Tör's cargo ship had been moored up – the one which had rescued her and Bear and taken them both to safety. Where once its gunmetal grey hull had sat proudly in the dock, now the quayside was empty.

She drew a sharp intake of breath. Because this was also the very same spot where she had walked off the boat with Bear by her side.

And just there – April hardly dared look – was the place where Lisé had taken the photo of the pair of them, the one she still kept close to her heart. But also, the place she had whispered her last goodbyes. She stared for the longest of times. Almost as if she could see the ghost of her former self still standing there. Half believing that if she stared long enough Bear might miraculously appear out of the sea fog. Rearing up on his hind legs and then galloping towards her, full pelt—

'Shall we take a look around?' Dad asked, flicking on his torch with a beam of sudden, bright light.

April nodded, clearing her head of the ghosts. 'Yes, of course.'

In the eerie light, there wasn't much to see. Unlike ports back home, which usually hummed with workers, tourists and fishermen, this was empty save for a few warehouse buildings. Even though she knew Tör probably had already left, she still felt disappointed. The only ships docked were a couple of hardy expedition boats with steel-enforced hulls – vessels strong enough to cope with the extreme weather conditions this far north and capable of breaking through compacted sea ice. But of any living thing – there was not a single sign.

'I'm here, Bear,' April whispered. 'I'm back.'

In the deepest chambers of her heart – where all her secrets lived – April had occasionally entertained a dream of what would happen when she returned to Svalbard. In this fantasy, Bear would somehow *know* she was back. She wouldn't have to search for him. He would just somehow be there and then they would run to each other and let out an almighty roar of reunion.

She listened carefully. Anything for a clue that he might be out there. That he knew she had returned. But no matter how hard she strained her ears, she heard nothing apart from the screeching of gulls and the hiss of the ocean.

'APRIL!' Dad yelled. 'OVER HERE!'

April froze. Not because of the cold, but from something far worse. There was a frightening urgency to his voice. A tone which sent a shiver of a different kind down her spine. She spun round to find him crouched on his haunches, his torch beam settled on a patch of something dark on the snow.

'Here!' Dad called again and her gut squirmed.

April somehow found her feet. One clumsy, heavy step after another until finally, she came to stand by Dad's shoulder. Her breath was tight in her throat and she forced herself to look down.

There, caught in a beam of light, was a stain of something unmistakable. Rusty red in the snow.

Blood.

Chapter Eight

The Polar Institute

April was vaguely aware of Dad pulling her away from the port, all the time reassuring her that the blood might be connected to something entirely different. He guided them to a large, L-shaped building about five minutes' walk away. The Polar Institute. Designed as a centre of scientific study and enquiry into the Arctic, it was where Lisé worked and the next logical place to try and get some answers.

April fumbled with the door but her fingers were so cold, she couldn't even turn the handle and it was Dad who ushered the pair of them inside to a brightly lit foyer, its white walls adorned with breathtaking photographs of the Arctic. In any other circumstances, April would have gazed around her in awe.

But not today.

Instead, she marched up to the counter where an older man with Afro hair and black glasses was busy typing into a laptop. He had a name badge above his left breast pocket which read 'Vincent'.

'Can I help?' He looked up, and then blinked a couple of times in surprise. April didn't know whether it was because of her age, her appearance or the fierceness of her expression. Quite possibly, it was all three.

'I'm looking for Lisé,' she said without bothering to introduce herself, but instead planting her hands on the counter. 'She's got purple hair and rainbow boots.'

'Ah! You mean Lisé Le Page.' Vincent nodded sagely. 'I'm afraid she left this morning on a field expedition to Friesland, in the north part of Svalbard. We have some quite remarkable conservation work going on up there—'

'She's *gone*?' April turned to her father in horror, who gulped rather loudly himself.

Up until this moment, she hadn't realised how much hope she'd pinned on talking to Lisé. Apart from Tör, she was the one person who could help them understand this harsh new world – who might have been able to provide some kind of assistance. 'But . . . but for how long?'

'Four weeks. Maybe longer. Depends on the variable weather conditions of course. She's part of a research group monitoring the birthing dens.' Vincent shrugged. 'These things don't work to a timetable as you can imagine.'

April nodded dully. She had read about such research trips. It was just one part of the important work the Polar Institute and various other charities and organisations were doing in the Arctic region – by monitoring the polar bear birthing dens and in particular, the fragile first few weeks and months of a cub's life, they could see how the polar bear population was being impacted by climate change and other human influences.

But whilst that was all Hugely Important, it didn't help right now.

April read the same frustration on her father's face. If only they had arrived sooner. She rubbed her eyes furiously.

'Can I help with anything?' Vincent asked, politely directing his gaze away from April and towards her father.

Dad cleared his throat. 'Yes, perhaps you can. We are looking for any information regarding the polar bear which potentially got injured the other evening in the port.'

'Ah, yes. An unfortunate but thankfully extremely rare incident. It appears some tourists accidentally unloaded their firearm.'

'Unfortunate indeed,' Dad replied wryly.

'And the bear?' April asked, trying her hardest to keep her voice steady. 'Was *he* injured?'

'We assume so but we cannot be sure of the severity. By the time the authorities had arrived, the bear had gone.'

'But . . . but gone *where*? Did anyone try looking for him?' April said. 'What will happen if . . . if he's badly hurt? Who would be there to help him?'

Vincent sighed. Not an unkind sigh, but more of weariness in the face of so many quick-fire enquiries.

'Like most children these days, my daughter cares about wildlife,' Dad said, curling a protective arm around April's shoulders. 'If there is anything at all you can tell us about the bear, it would greatly put our minds at ease.'

Vincent adjusted his glasses and looked at Dad properly for the first time since they had arrived. 'I don't believe I took your name?'

'Edmund Wood,' Dad replied. 'And my daughter, April.'

'April, did you say? *April Wood?*' Vincent snapped shut his laptop. 'Not THE April Wood?'

April swallowed nervously. Her palms were still flat on the counter and in the reflection of Vincent's glasses, she could see a blotchy-faced girl with hair sticking up at right angles. She was suddenly and very starkly aware she hadn't shown her best side.

Just as she was about to apologise for barging in, Vincent jumped to his feet and pumped her hand vigorously. 'I wasn't working at the Institute at the time but I heard about you. We all did. They told me your age but I must confess, I did not realise you were quite so young.'

By now, April was used to grown-ups looking at her in surprise and how they often underestimated how much someone so little could achieve. It was especially annoying when grown-ups always overestimated how much *they* could achieve.

'Young, but extraordinarily brave,' Dad said, tightening his arm around April's shoulders.

'You think it is the same bear?' Vincent stared at April. 'Is that why you are here?'

April squirmed. She hadn't thought through what she would say if she talked to anyone other than Lisé. She hadn't thought through *anything*. Save for following the wild, pure fury that had pulled her and her father here. But barely twelve hours into their mission, and it was already starting to feel much harder than she had ever imagined.

'We have reason to believe it might be so,' Dad said cautiously.

Vincent raised an enquiring eyebrow.

'He was standing on his two hind legs and roaring in the port. It was what he did when we said goodbye. It was what he *always* did,' April said, and was about to say more when she noticed Vincent's expression.

'Didn't you also give him a name? I seem to recall?'

'Bear,' she said quietly.

'*Bear*,' Vincent repeated. 'How extraordinary.'

April wanted to say it wasn't extraordinary. That

in fact, making friends with Bear had been the most natural, wonderful thing in the whole wide world. And that unlike making friends with humans, it wasn't difficult – it was easy and effortless and so beautiful it still made her heart ache.

But she said none of that. Not because she didn't want to but because of the way Vincent was now looking at her.

'If it is the same bear, then regardless of the bond you once had, I do not recommend under any circumstances trying to find him,' he warned. 'Not least because it will be impossible – do you know how large an area the Svalbard archipelago covers? It would be like looking for a needle in a haystack. And if he has been injured, then he will be extremely dangerous. There have been increasing incidents of polar bear attacks on humans.'

'Only because they're starving!' April retorted angrily. 'Not because they want to. It's because they're forced to go near humans to try and find food!'

'That is quite so,' Vincent nodded. 'But you can see the risk?'

'Bear wouldn't hurt me,' April said. 'I just know it.'

'Yes, but . . . ' Vincent's voice tailed off.

'But *what*?'

He looked at her again and it was then April placed the expression in his eyes. It was not wonder or awe or even disbelief. It was a look of pure pity. 'But you are missing one crucial fact,' he said softly. 'What if the bear doesn't remember you at all?'

CHAPTER NINE

A Frosty Encounter

'No!' THE CRY was so guttural, April wasn't even sure it had come from her. She turned on her heel and raced out of the door.

'APRIL!' Dad cried.

Without even looking back, she took off down the pavement, Vincent's words ringing in her ears.

Of course, Bear wasn't a pet. He was a wild animal. A wild animal who had been returned to his natural habitat. And in this stark new world, it was more than possible he might have forgotten his brief encounter with a human.

Even a human who loved him as much as she did.

Is *that* why he hadn't appeared yet? Because he didn't even know who she was any more? Because he had forgotten her?

She swallowed back a rising sob. She knew Vincent hadn't meant to be hurtful. For someone who lived and worked in Svalbard, he had merely been pointing out the practical considerations. Not just about whether Bear would remember her, but also how difficult it would be to find out what had happened to him.

But there was no way she could give up looking for him. Not having seen that blood. She could *never* give up. Not until she knew he was safe.

'Bear!' she shouted, slipping and sliding along the

snow, only stopping periodically to wipe the snot from her nose. 'BEAR!'

She called out his name again and again. Her voice increasingly more desperate. Hoping that somewhere out there he would be able to hear her. That he would come loping down the street and envelop her in the biggest of bear hugs and make everything all right again.

By now she had shouted herself hoarse and she slid to a halt, her chest heaving and her breath ragged. She cast a wild glance around her. Where was she? The main street? Or somewhere else. That was the hill, wasn't it? The one with their hotel. But it didn't look familiar at all.

'Oh no.'

Somehow, unknowingly, she had ended up on the outskirts of the town – where the few houses there were petered out and the vast Arctic tundra began. Here, even the air smelled different – wilder, more intense, dangerous somehow.

A thick cloud gathered ominously above her and immediately the temperature dipped. To make matters worse, huge craggy flakes of snow started to drift down from the sky. A thousand thoughts flashed through her mind. If only she had listened to Dad and gone shopping for proper winter clothes. If only she hadn't just run off. If only she had thought to bring the map.

April felt a horrible flush of shame. Shame and something else – the sting of disappointment in herself.

'What are you doing here?'

The voice came out of nowhere, making April jump. She lost her footing, slipping off the kerb and tumbling into a deep pocket of snow. By the time she had wiped the snow from her face and peered upwards, she was looking into the face of an old lady with huge grey eyes and skin as weathered as leather. She was wearing fleece-lined snow boots and an ankle-length coat that seemed to be made of patchwork pieces of felt and various other materials with a thick, lined hood. Behind her, she pulled a red sled.

'I-I-I . . . I,' April tried to speak but couldn't. Her teeth were chattering far too much for any words to come out. Instead, she flushed bright pink under the older woman's piercing gaze. She slowly rose to her feet and tried not to shiver.

'Can't you see the sign?' The woman tutted and pointed to a red warning sign indicating polar bears. 'You tourists come to this part of the world and yet do not stop to realise how much danger you are in.'

April wanted to say many things, but under the woman's sharp frown they all withered and died on her tongue. One thing was for sure – she definitely wasn't going to admit that she was searching for a polar bear.

'H-h-how can I get back to my hotel?' she asked instead.

'Not by walking. Not in those shoes anyway,' the woman replied.

Before April could answer, the lady shook her head in disapproval, before removing her coat and passing it to April. 'Take this,' she said curtly.

April wrapped it around herself gratefully, soaking in the instant warmth it provided. The coat smelled strange and comforting at the same time – with the strong scent of something musky and feral.

'I . . . I'd better head back,' she said, looking towards town, which suddenly seemed an awfully long way away.

'I will take you.'

Then before April knew what was happening, the older woman somehow single-handedly manoeuvred her on to the sled. Without stopping to pause, she tied the sled cord round her waist, strapped a pair of skis to her feet and set off down the street.

April hadn't been on a sled since Bear Island. It was one of the things she missed about her summer there.

But this sled ride was different. It wasn't fun or frivolous or silly. During the whole journey the old lady didn't speak once except to ask the name of April's hotel.

By the time they arrived at the entrance, she wasn't even out of breath despite the fact she had been pulling the sled mostly uphill.

'Foolish, irresponsible child,' she muttered, and without waiting for thanks she yanked open the hotel door. 'I suggest you get inside. Or better still return home where you belong.'

Chapter Ten

Surprise

It took a few minutes once April was safely inside the warm hotel foyer to stop shivering. But what felt worse than the cold was the sting of the older lady's words.

Yes, she had been rude.

But she had also been *right*.

Like some kind of superhero, April had rushed to

Svalbard thinking she could rescue Bear. But what had happened? She had ended up having to be rescued herself on the very first day. On the wall, the reindeer head gazed at her forlornly.

'I'm sorry, Hamish,' she whispered.

She didn't know why she was apologising to him, but in the absence of Bear she needed someone or some*thing* to say sorry to.

It was clear Bear was no longer in town, which could only mean one thing – he was somewhere in the vast wilderness of Svalbard. She had only experienced it for a millisecond but it was enough to appreciate how dangerous this part of the Arctic could potentially be. This was no Bear Island in summer. Svalbard was much, much larger – an area covering 24,000 square miles and ninety-nine per cent of it complete, unfiltered wilderness. The name itself even meant 'Cold Shores'. Made up of glaciers, fjords and ice caves it was so dry, it was actually classified as a desert, which was why it was also referred to as a tundra. There was no way she would be able to find him, let alone know where to even start looking. Not in the thick of winter. Especially not alone.

Even Hamish's immobile face seemed to agree it was a preposterous idea.

It was at that moment the door opened and the wintry air rushed in. April braced herself. No doubt it was the woman come to give her another scolding and remind her that tourists didn't belong here.

'April Wood! There you are.'

But no. It wasn't the old woman.

It wasn't the old woman at all.

Even though April had her back to the door, she stiffened. Because she knew that clipped voice. But still she hardly dared believe it. She spun round, her eyes widening in shock and then excitement.

'*Tör?!*'

He stood in the doorway, dressed in red snow boots and a jet-black ski suit, with a pair of skis in one hand that were dripping snow on to the floor. His goggles rested on his fair hair and his eyes shone as bright as any sun.

April opened her mouth, closed it again, before eventually finding her tongue. 'But . . . what are you doing here?'

'Isn't it obvious?' he said, propping the skis up against the wall. 'I'm looking for you. Something I seem to do a lot of.'

He took a tentative step forward and then halted as they awkwardly gazed at one other. They had written so often, that to be together in person felt quite strange. As if they needed to recalibrate to the real-life version of each other. But then he held out his hand and she grasped it. It felt like old rope. Safe and comforting. A hand that could always pull her out of trouble.

Close up she could see how Tör had grown – he was now a full head above her – and his face was leaner and more angular. But, as he flashed her a familiar grin, she was relieved to see he was still the same slightly mischievous boy he had always been.

'I'm *so* glad you're here.'

Tör was about to reply when the door burst open again, and this time it was her father who tumbled through, quickly followed by Jurgen.

'April! Thank goodness. You're safe!' Her father grabbed her by the shoulders and pressed her tightly to his chest, where she could hear the thud of his heart ticking like a racing clock. When he finally released her, April noticed he was swaddled up in Arctic clothing, as if he were about to head off on an expedition to the North Pole. But more strangely than that, he didn't seem at all surprised to see Tör.

'*Dad? Tör?*'

'I sense there is some catching up to do,' Jurgen said, reading the confusion on her face. 'Do come with me. It is much warmer in my room.'

The four of them passed through the door marked 'Private' and into Jurgen's living space. It was surprisingly well-furnished and April was relieved to see no taxidermised animal heads. The room had warm comfortable sofas, an old grandfather clock and a sideboard full of photos of a young girl slightly older than April.

'My daughter, Svetlana,' he said, catching April's gaze. 'Let me prepare some hot drinks. Please make yourselves at home.'

Jurgen disappeared and April curled up on the sofa closest to the fire, her fingers and toes slowly creeping back to life. Whilst she warmed up, Dad and Tör took turns filling her in.

'You ran out of the Polar Institute and I had no idea where you had gone,' Dad started. He was pacing up and down on the rug in front of the fire. 'I went out to try to find you and that was when I bumped into Tör.'

'I'm sorry I just ran off,' April said. 'It was wrong of me.'

Dad patted her hand clumsily to let her know she was forgiven, and Tör took up the next part of the story.

'You never told me which hotel you were staying in, so I went to every place in town before I decided to try the Polar Institute. I had just got there when your father burst out of the door saying he had lost you.'

'We looked up and down the street but couldn't find you anywhere,' Dad added. 'Then Tör insisted on bringing me back to the hotel where Jurgen lent me some of his clothes, and the three of us began a search party.'

'I thought you had left on the boat?' April said, turning to Tör.

'My father wanted me to return to the mainland of Norway.' Tör shrugged. 'But how could I? This part of the world – even after your summer on Bear Island – it is not what you are used to. I thought you could use some extra help.'

Her father seemed about to say something but cleared his throat instead. April sensed he was going to mention what Vincent had said in the Institute.

'Even if Bear doesn't remember me,' she said, lifting her chin defiantly, 'I'd still rescue him a thousand times over. Because that's what we're meant to do, isn't it?'

'*We?*' Dad asked.

'Humans!' April answered, somewhat exasperated at always having to point out the obvious. 'We are supposed to take care of animals. But we don't.'

'And that is exactly why I told your father that he must allow you to continue your search.'

'*Dad!*' April growled. 'You weren't going to take me home, were you? Not after everything you said before we came here?!'

Dad had the courtesy to blush. 'It's only because as your father I worry about you. I simply want you to be safe. But then Tör reminded me that you'd never forgive me if I took you home now.'

'He's right,' April said. 'I can't just leave Bear. You know I can't.'

'I am aware of that now,' Dad sighed. 'And truth be told, I feel a lot happier that Tör is here to help us. But April, you mustn't go running off again. Do you promise me?'

Dad looked so tired, a crease of worry etched between his brows, that April felt her tummy squirm in guilt. She knew he was just concerned about her, especially as being here probably brought back memories of her near-drowning. It brought back those memories for her too. 'I promise.'

'Good. We are all on the same page,' Tör said brightly. 'So, what do we know so far?'

Dad and April filled Tör in on what they had discovered since arriving last night – which admittedly wasn't an awful lot.

'I also have done a little research,' Tör said. 'There is a strong female polar bear population just north of the Widjefjord in Friesland.'

'Where Lisé is!'

'But, after further investigation, I have realised it is too far for an injured bear to travel.'

'In other words, he must be fairly close by still,' Dad said.

'Which leads us to Sabine Land,' Tör replied. 'On the east coast of Svalbard. It is not so far away and apparently there have been recent sightings of male polar bears in the area.'

'You think Bear might have gone there?' April asked hopefully.

'It is the most logical lead we have,' Tör shrugged.

'It's the *only* lead we have,' Dad replied, frowning.

'Which means we have to go looking for him,' April declared. 'We have to go there!'

'Yes, but in order to do that, we must be prepared, April,' Dad said in a voice which had resigned itself to the inevitable.

'Your father is correct,' Tör said. 'We must equip ourselves with the appropriate clothes, cold weather equipment, but most of all we must find a guide. I know Longyearbyen, but that is all. We need someone who knows the tundra like the back of their hand. Someone who can help us find Bear.'

At which point, there was a massive clatter in the doorway as Jurgen dropped his tray of drinks everywhere. 'You are searching for a missing polar bear?'

CHAPTER ELEVEN

Preparation

AFTER THE SPILLED drinks had been mopped up, and Jurgen had been trusted with an explanation, his eyes lit up with a feverish excitement.

'You actually rescued a polar bear?' he exclaimed. 'I knew there was something different about you. It is in the eyes, you know. I can always tell. Oh, Svetlana would have loved this! She had a soft spot for the bears. Said we needed to look after them better. And you say you are going to hunt for him?'

'Not *hunt*,' April answered, thinking of poor Hamish. 'Search.'

'Of course, of course. But if you don't mind me saying so, you are not thinking of going by yourselves, are you?'

'Naturally we will need assistance,' Dad said. 'Perhaps you can recommend someone?'

'Of course! I know of the perfect person! The community here is so small we know what each other has had for breakfast before we have even eaten it ourselves.' Jurgen chuckled at his own joke, before opening one of the cabinet drawers and pulling out a glass jar full of sweets. 'Aniseed candy anyone? An acquired taste but one I am rather fond of.'

'Oh!' Dad exclaimed. 'Don't mind if I do.'

'*And?*' April said, trying not to sound impatient. 'The person you are thinking of?'

'Ah,' Jurgen replied. 'Her name is Hedda. A woman of few words. She probably talks to her dogs more than she does humans. But a true soul of the Arctic who comes from a long history of trackers.'

'Trackers?' April asked, her own eyes lighting up. Because she knew exactly what a tracker was. She had a whole page dedicated to them in her diary. A tracker was a person who followed animal trails – scents, pawprints, discarded pieces of fur . . . poo even. In the olden days, trackers were also hunters, but these days they were mostly tour guides or gamekeepers.

'She runs a husky dog business – taking tourists for dog sled rides. Quite a common activity here as you can imagine,' Jurgen said. 'She knows the eastern region of Sabine Land better than anyone round here. If anyone can help you, it is Hedda. But a word of caution, I probably wouldn't tell her you are searching for a missing bear.'

'Why not?' April asked. 'Surely it would be easier and more honest if she knew?'

'Because most people in these parts believe that bears should be kept well away from human settlements,' Jurgen said slowly, as if carefully choosing his words. 'And some people, like Hedda, think it is only a matter of time before someone gets hurt. She would not approve of you trying to get close to one.'

'Is there no one else that can help?' Dad asked.

'No one as experienced as Hedda, no.'

Tör, April and her father all looked at each other before finally nodding.

'Then I will arrange it for you,' Jurgen said, rubbing his hands together in excitement. 'I will say you are seeking a tourist adventure – a sled ride under the northern lights! She will not suspect anything different.'

Hedda had been reluctant at such short notice, but thanks to a favour she apparently owed Jurgen, she agreed to take the three of them on a three-night winter excursion to the east coast of Svalbard, under the pretext of looking at the northern lights.

They would set off early the following morning.

As Jurgen put the phone down and confirmed the details, April felt a frisson of wonder pass through her. Partly for the adventure which lay ahead. Partly for the journey into the unknown. But most of all, for the possibility of finding Bear.

All that was left to do now was get ready.

Luckily Jurgen had said Dad could borrow his clothes for the expedition, including a pair of snow boots that fitted even his imperfectly sized feet. Tör was already fully equipped. That just left April.

'You will freeze to death!' Tör said, shaking his head.

'I knew we should have gone earlier,' Dad muttered. 'The expedition shop will be closed by now.'

'Hmmm. I might be able to help,' Jurgen said, narrowing his eyes as he looked at April. He beckoned her to follow him into a compact utility room, next to the foyer, which was crammed to the brim with outdoor clothes and snow equipment. 'This is Svetlana's,' he said, pointing to some smaller-sized clothing in the corner.

'I . . . keep it here for when she comes to visit. You are most welcome to it.'

'You'll really let me borrow this?'

'Svetlana would want you to have it,' Jurgen replied, giving April a sad smile.

A smile that April recognised because it was the empty smile of someone who is pretending not to be lonely.

'Her mother is an engineer,' Jurgen said, fiddling with his timepiece. 'In the end, she wanted more than this tiny community could offer her. But for Svetlana . . . well, this was her home. Anyway, you are about the same size,' he said, shaking off the sadness before placing item after item in April's outstretched arms including base layers, waterproofs, fleeces, an ankle-length padded coat, two pairs of gloves, a felt-lined bobble hat, a warm scarf and some snow goggles. Finally, off a hook, he gently pulled a cream round-neck sweater, woven in the finest merino wool and decorated with a neat row of polar bears. He handed it over. 'This

was her favourite. I know she would like you to have it.'

After Jurgen had gone, and April had got dressed, she stared at herself in the mirror. She looked three sizes larger than her previous self. But, for the first time since arriving in the Arctic, she also felt ready for the size of the task ahead.

Well, *almost* ready.

Jurgen, Dad and Tör entered and April turned to them worriedly.

'I don't have any snow boots!'

'Oh wait,' Jurgen said. 'Svetlana bought these last winter but left them behind.'

He busied himself in some cardboard boxes on the floor, before handing one over.

April peeled off the lid, sensing the others' hushed gaze upon on her.

Inside were a pair of fleece-lined rainbow boots.

CHAPTER TWELVE

Hedda

Early the next morning, long before the sun had woken, they boarded Jurgen's snowmobile and headed over to Hedda's cabin. April heard the yapping, snarling and barking of the huskies even before he had cut the engine. Located beyond the polar bear warning sign, it was constructed from strong timber with its frontside facing the wilderness, as if keeping guard against all that lay beyond. Unlike some of the other cabins they had passed on the way, which were warm and homely, with sweet-smelling smoke billowing out of their chimneys and even the occasional chintz curtains, this one was stark and angular and shrouded in darkness. There was a tangled pile of reindeer antlers and some dried fish hanging from the porch.

'Is anyone in?' Dad asked anxiously.

'Only one way to find out!'

Despite the butterflies in her tummy, April marched up to the front door and lifted the heavy iron knocker, cast in the shape of a husky's face. As she dropped it on the thick wooden door, the clanging set the dogs off into another frenzy of barking. The others gathered behind her and all of them watched as the door slowly creaked open.

One look at the face peering out of the door and April's heart sank. Of all her luck! It was the same woman as yesterday.

'*Hedda?*' she gulped.

'You!' the old woman muttered.

'You two have already met?' Jurgen asked.

'Briefly,' Hedda replied curtly.

'Well, allow me to introduce you properly. This is April, her father Edmund, and finally, Tör,' Jurgen said. 'Hedda shall be your guide to Sabine Land.'

Hedda turned her gaze slowly from person to person, before finally resting it upon April. It was a fierce, searching gaze. And not a particularly friendly one.

'You did not tell me there was a child in the party,' she said, frowning. 'I cannot possibly take her into the tundra at this time of year. It is far too dangerous.'

April pulled herself to her full height and looked Hedda directly in the eyes. They were the colour of wolf fur and storm clouds. 'I am not afraid of danger.'

If she thought this would have the desired effect, she was wrong. Hedda let out a bark of laughter. 'That is very admirable, but the Arctic is the biggest test of all. It does not care about the emotions in your heart, it does not care how strong you are, it does not even care about how much money you have. It only cares for one thing – whether you have it within you to survive the harshest, most inhospitable place on Earth. And you have already proven you are not up to the challenge.' Hedda went to close the door.

'Then it is clear you do not know my daughter,' Dad said, putting his foot inside the door and preventing it from closing. 'Because if you did, then you would know she is the bravest person out of all of us here.'

Hedda narrowed her eyes but said nothing.

'Let me prove myself,' April said quietly. '*Please?*'

Still Hedda said nothing. April's heart raced – pitter-pattering against her chest. They had come so far. It would be the cruellest of luck to fail now.

'Fine, I will take you. But not for three nights. Only two. That is my final offer.'

After making sure Hedda wasn't going to change her mind, Jurgen bid them goodbye – but not before giving

Dad a stash of aniseed candy and April a bag of peanuts.

'For energy,' he said, climbing back up on to his snowmobile. 'I shall see you on your return. Your successful return!'

Once he had sped off, Hedda guided them to the dog yard which sat directly behind her cabin. April's eyes lit up. She had never seen so many dogs in one place! Encased by a high wire fence, the yard housed at least thirty wooden kennels on stilts, each one home to a beautiful husky dog – some dark brown, some the colour of moon silver, others a mix of the two. Each kennel had a different name marked on it. Nearest to her was a ginormous brown dog called Bo and, unable to resist, she gave him a gentle pat on the head.

After explaining that huskies were different from pet dogs back home because of their endurance and ability to withstand the cold, Hedda beckoned everyone close to her.

'There are three main rules for you to follow,' she commanded, taking position by a kennel marked with the name 'Ripley'. 'Rule number one and the most important of all: do not go wandering off alone. You do not want to get lost in the Arctic because it is very likely you will never be found again. At least not alive anyway,' Hedda pulled a grim smile. 'Once we leave town, you must stay with your sled at all times. Is that understood? The dogs know the area far better than you do and are trained to take you to safety.'

April snuck a look across at Dad, whose face had paled considerably.

'Rule number two,' Hedda continued. 'If we see a polar bear, you *do not* approach it. There are strict safety rules about polar bears in Svalbard and it is imperative that you follow them.'

April opened her mouth to retort but a sharp elbow in the ribs from Tör made her swiftly close it again. Instead, she clenched her fists by her side and bristled.

'Rule number three?' asked her father, his Adam's apple bobbing nervously up and down. 'You said there were three rules.'

'Rule number three.' Hedda gazed at all of them in turn. 'Always make sure you tie the dogs up properly when you stop.'

Once she seemed satisfied they had got the message, she proceeded to the practical instructions on how to ride the sled, including how the steerer needed to keep their feet on the brake at all times when stationary. As she spoke, the dogs twisted and turned in excitement, tails wagging and eyes shining at the prospect of an adventure.

'The number of dogs depends on the weight of the sled. But typically we need two wheel dogs, a larger amount of pack dogs and then a lead dog. All of them work as a team, but without the lead dog, the pack will pull in many different directions and end up going nowhere. It is the lead dog that must be brave enough to carve the route to give the others the courage to follow.'

'But how do you choose the lead dog?' April asked curiously.

Hedda cast her a withering look. 'The way you

choose all leaders. They choose themselves. Now let us not waste any more time.'

Hedda then barked out instructions to get the sleds ready. As well as equipment such as sleeping bags, thermal rugs and tents, there was also a large amount of cooking gear, food and water for themselves and the dogs, plus medical supplies. Most of this Hedda had already packed so it was mostly about tightening straps and making sure everything was in place.

Dad and Hedda were to ride together on one sled, being led by a lively looking Ripley, with April and Tör on the other. The lead dog for their sled was Finnegan, who had burnished silver fur and intelligent blue eyes. April was happy to see that Bo was also on her team.

'The dogs in the trail sled are trained to follow the lead sled, but in case you get into any difficulty there is a safety pack on your sled which contains a satellite phone, a knife, a whistle and a flare gun, as well as emergency provisions of food, water and clothing plus means of lighting a fire.'

Hedda disappeared into the house before exiting with an axe under one arm, a flare gun and most alarmingly of all, a rifle.

April gulped. She knew it was a legal requirement to carry a firearm in Svalbard but seeing it with her own eyes sent a jolt to her tummy.

But she didn't have time to be alarmed for long, because the sleds had been tripled-checked by Hedda and the dogs harnessed. There were nine dogs on Tör and April's sled and eleven pulling Hedda and Dad's, each one straining at the harness and barking loudly. With the sun due to rise any minute, it was finally time to go.

Behind Hedda, April caught a glimpse of her father's pale face. She wanted to call out and reassure him, but by now the dogs were so loud she could barely hear herself think.

'MUSH!' Hedda called.

The dogs on both sleds snapped and snarled and suddenly tore forward in a burst of strength and power. They were off.

April looked behind her one last time and saw the bright lights of the town gradually fade until the last light disappeared and darkness descended like a hush. In mere minutes, the settlement, and all its comfort and safety, had been left behind.

And the true Arctic adventure had begun.

Chapter Thirteen

Husky Ride

By the growing sunlight, the track the dogs initially followed seemed well-worn. They were passing through the neck of a valley, with mountains rearing up on either side of them. Not that April dared to look up much.

Tör had been husky riding many times before in

mainland Norway but insisted April pilot the sled to gain experience. Even though she kept her knees bent as Hedda had instructed, it was far harder than it looked and it took all of her strength and concentration just to stay upright. She had never been skiing, wasn't much good at ice-skating and she wasn't used to holding such a fixed posture. Her arms were stiff and her hands clenched on tight to the bar. Too tight. The dogs could sense her discomfort and began to lose the shape of the line.

'Sorry,' she murmured. 'I know I just need to relax.'

'Soften your limbs!' Tör yelled into her ear over the wind. 'Remember what you once told me? Imagine you are like water.'

Despite the fact she couldn't see Tör's face, she smiled anyway as she pictured their very first meeting on the boat – when she had given him advice on how to stay relaxed around animals. She imagined her limbs softening, like a tree in a breeze, and roots from her feet travelling down into the earth. After a while April began to soften into the sensation. Of holding on to the handlebar – tightly but not too tightly. Of becoming one with nature.

Because if there was anything April Wood could do well – it was this.

With her insulated clothes and fleece-lined boots, she felt protected against the sting of the cold. The wind

rushed past her ears, the blades of the sled swished on the snow and the vast sky yawned overhead. She relaxed the tension out of her legs and arms, feeling the fluidity of the movement course through her. For a brief, dazzling moment, it was as if she were an extension of the husky team – not standing on the sled but one of the pack, racing across the Arctic.

The moment ended abruptly when Bo and Coco – the two wheel dogs – got distracted by the looseness in her grasp, sensing that her focus had shifted away from them. The lines tangled and before she knew it, she was face down in the snow.

'You must work with the dogs, April,' Hedda called sharply from her own sled. 'You cannot expect them to do all the work for you.'

April flushed under the reprimand. Despite a knock to her knee, she climbed back on and for the next few hours, focused on nothing but the dogs, staying in a state of relaxed tension. Onwards they travelled through troughs and valleys, surrounded by steep mountain peaks on all sides.

It wasn't like back home, where the landscape would be punctuated by the occasional tree, hedgerow or even a row of houses. This was still and bare and void of any life. Even with all the snow, it was clear no plants or trees or any noticeable vegetation grew here.

And even though April had been to the Arctic before,

it was then she realised she had not really experienced the *true* Arctic. Not like this. The Arctic in winter was not a friendly, welcoming place. It was an immense, silent world full of strange, distorted shadows and made up of a landscape that didn't even seem to belong on Earth at all.

Apart from the panting of the dogs, the two sleds travelled in silence, seeing nothing but their own shadows. It was hard, exhausting work and every muscle in April's body ached. Come lunchtime, she tumbled off the sled and sank into a relieved crouch.

'You must feed the dogs, unclip the harness, remove any ice and change their socks. On my trips, the dogs always come first,' Hedda commanded everyone.

April immediately felt guilty. Even though the huskies loved long-distance running, it was still important to look after them. She gave each of the dogs in her team some fuss and whispered a thank you into their ears. Only once they had all been fed, watered and arranged in a protective circle around the group, did

Hedda finally take out their provisions. First up, there was some warm vegetarian soup served with thick rye bread. 'Here,' Hedda offered once the soup had been eaten. 'Dried reindeer meat.'

'No, thank you.' Instead, April pulled out her packet of peanuts and nibbled on those instead.

'There is a cabin about three hours from here,' Hedda said. 'We will head there and rest for the night.'

Whilst the dogs took a quick nap, their tails twitching in their dreams, Hedda retreated into silence, staring into the distance with a cautious expression on her face. Her axe rested across her knees and the flare gun and rifle lay to her side.

April knew what she was guarding against. But still, she couldn't resist asking.

'What are you looking for?'

'Keeping watch for polar bears.'

April knew the flare gun wouldn't hurt a bear. With its loud noise, it was simply intended to frighten them. But if that didn't work, then . . .

'You shoot them in the heart,' Hedda said as if reading her mind.

Chapter Fourteen

Chocolate and Change

THE CABIN, ALTHOUGH sparse, was surprisingly cosy. It was made of wood, smelled of campfires and was located in the middle of absolutely nowhere. Once upon a time it was used by hunters, otherwise known as trappers, who would spend the long winters in Svalbard catching seals, foxes and polar bears for their pelts. These days, its use was for much more benign reasons – providing shelter to those brave or foolhardy enough to travel across the Arctic terrain.

Despite the fact Hedda had barely said three words all day other than to shout orders and point out the occasional reindeer or fox track, April had to admire the woman's ability to navigate them here. Unlike back home, there were no signposts, no roads, no obvious markers – just layers of thick compacted snow and, since the brief winter sun had already set, the faint overhead glisten of stars.

When the two sleds finally pulled up, April was so tired she could barely walk. But by now they all knew the drill. The dogs had to be fed and watered first and, since it was evening, they had to make sure they were settled for the night. Meanwhile Hedda had grabbed her pickaxe and was busy shovelling the fresh snow away from the door.

Inside was spartan but welcoming. There were two solid planks of wood nailed to one wall which April presumed were beds, a small metal stove in the centre of the room and various ice picks, axes and cooking instruments hanging from hooks on the walls. It was cold though. Very cold. So the first thing Hedda did was light the stove.

'You see how it is already prepared?' she said to the group who stood around it in such exhaustion, that not one of them could even muster a reply. 'That is one of the rules in Svalbard. Always leave the cabin ready for the next traveller.'

Hedda asked Tör to fill a red kettle with snow since he was the most alert of the three. As he left the cabin, and Hedda busied herself with emptying her pack, Dad sank wearily to his haunches. 'Are you okay?' April whispered. He hadn't said anything for hours and looked ever so slightly shell-shocked. 'Maybe a nice cup of tea?'

Dad nodded quietly. April didn't think she'd ever seen him look so miserable. 'I don't suppose they have a record player in here, do they?'

Despite the circumstances, April burst into laughter.

The sound was so sudden and loud, that it bounced around the cabin like thunder. Hedda frowned.

'What are you doing?' At first April thought she was addressing her, but Hedda's sharp gaze was fixed on her father, who had slumped to the floor.

'Resting a weary soul,' Dad replied.

'You must get changed first,' she instructed. 'We have to clean our boots, remove any wet clothing and change into our warm clothes. Actions like these are what save your life out here. When you can't be bothered, that is when you must be the most bothered.'

Dad sighed. April knew Hedda was right, but she wished she could be a bit nicer with it. She squeezed Dad's hand and hoped he got the significance. After all, it hadn't exactly been his choice to come on this adventure.

Once the fire was fully ablaze, the four of them sat around it drinking in the warmth gratefully. Hedda had repeatedly warned them against the dangers of polar bears smelling food, and since they were nearing the polar bear region, it was why she'd made sure everyone was safely inside the cabin with the doors sealed, before placing the kettle on the stove. Once the water had been boiled twice to make sure it was sterilised, Tör poured tea into steel mugs. April cradled her fingers round her mug and took a sip. She wasn't a fan of tea at the best of times, and this tasted weak and a bit coppery.

Maybe if she closed her eyes, she could imagine it was hot chocolate.

She could just about smell it. Sweet and sugary and milky. When she opened her eyes, she blinked in surprise. Hedda was holding a bar of chocolate and carefully breaking it into quarters. She passed the first piece to April.

'For you. You worked hard today.'

'Thank you!' she said, so surprised at the kind words she almost forgot how to speak.

Tör cut his quarter up into even pieces, eating one piece now and saving the rest for later. Hedda ate hers methodically, square by square, Dad gobbled his chocolate in one greedy go whilst April broke off a small chunk and popped it in her mouth. She sighed in contentment as it melted and decided she would save the rest for Bear.

That is, if he was okay. Despite listening out all day for any signs of him, she still hadn't heard anything. Her insides squiggled in response, the way they did before exams and long journeys. Suddenly the chocolate tasted bitter in her mouth.

'The skies are overcast so I do not think we will see any northern lights tonight,' Hedda said, interrupting her thoughts. 'But perhaps tomorrow if you are lucky.'

'I hope we get to see them,' Dad said dreamily, as if forgetting the real reason they were here. 'Do you remember the midnight sun, April?'

Despite the knots in her tummy, April smiled at the memory. Watching the midnight sun together had been one of the few moments of happiness she'd shared with her father on Bear Island. 'When the sun never goes to sleep and stays up all night.'

'Well, the northern lights are the opposite,' he replied, his own eyes lighting up. 'Although interestingly, the energy for making the lights comes from the sun. The sun creates solar wind, you see. In fact, the name Aurora Borealis, which is the scientific name for the northern lights, actually means "sunrise and wind".'

'I have seen them a few times,' said Tör. 'Each time it is something remarkable. Something truly everyone should experience.'

Even though April was here to find Bear, she sent out a little wish to the universe that she might also get to see these strange, miraculous lights too.

'One of nature's best gifts. One that even humankind cannot spoil.' Hedda let out a long sigh. 'Unlike the Arctic.'

'What changes have you seen?' asked Dad curiously. 'I spent the summer measuring temperatures on Bear Island. But I wonder how things have been affected this further north.'

'Too many I care to talk about,' said Hedda. 'The first thing is the rain. When I was younger we maybe had rain once, twice a year. But now? We see more and more rain every autumn. This is why we get landslides in Longyearbyen. It has always been a dangerous place to live. But these days it is dangerous for different reasons.' Hedda frowned. 'And I do not even wish to think about the added implications of permafrost melting.'

It was strange, April thought. Being here in winter it was hard to imagine that the Arctic was altering. That was the thing with climate change. So much of it was still so out of sight. But if anyone knew first-hand what was happening, it would be someone who had lived here for years and could see the effects with their own eyes.

'The fjords used to be completely frozen every winter,' Hedda said. 'But now many of them do not even freeze over. The glaciers are melting. The geese come earlier and leave later. There is even cod in the waters where there never used to be. And of course, there are the polar bears . . . '

She shook her head.

'I suggest it is now time for bed,' she said brusquely. 'The dogs will keep guard, but if you hear any strange noises in the night then whatever you do, do not go outside. Not even for the toilet.'

After a quick discussion, it was agreed that Dad and April would have the bunk beds, whilst Hedda and Tör would sleep wrapped in their sleeping bags, next to the stove.

As the others dropped off to sleep, April felt a shudder of excitement. As if there were lights inside her own belly – coursing through her and flickering their energy through her veins. Tomorrow they would reach Sabine Land. And that meant, paws crossed, they would find Bear.

There was no point thinking the worst. She had to believe that Bear was okay. She *had* to. Before falling asleep, she checked her pack. There at the bottom was the jar of peanut butter. She hugged the bag close, drifted off and dreamed of her best friend.

Chapter Fifteen

A Bear Roar

April woke in the middle of the night. The bed was like lying on concrete, and her left hip throbbed. Even with her eyes wide open, the cabin was pitch-black. The only sounds were the muffled snores of her father on the bottom bunk, and then closer to the stove the rhythmic breathing of the other two.

But that wasn't what had woken her up.

Because out there – through the wooden cabin walls – she could hear a *different* noise. A noise that thrummed each and every chord in her soul.

The noise of a polar bear.

She sat bolt upright and pressed her ear against the cabin wall, but the only thing she could hear through the thick wood was the vast aching silence of the Arctic pressing back.

For a brief moment, she wondered if she had dreamed it.

Just as she was about to lie back down – she caught the faintest rumble. Low, fierce and magnificent. Unmistakably a roar. But where was it coming from? Even with her sensitive hearing, in the weird way that sound travels in the Arctic, she had no idea if the noise was miles and miles away or right outside the cabin.

One thing she did know. She was going to find out.

April slipped out of her sleeping bag and carefully climbed down from the top bunk. She froze as someone stirred by the stove, then gradually tiptoed her way to the door. The noise came again, closer now. She cocked her ear to make sure. Yes, it was definitely a roar. Her heart skipped in response.

She paused by the door and took a deep breath. Not for courage. But to steady herself.

On the other side, she could hear the dogs stirring. One of them whined. And then something else – something which sounded like humungous heavy pawprints padding on the snow.

'*Bear?!*' she whispered, her nerves skittering this way and that.

She heard the noise again. Closer this time. Oh, Bear.

He was out there! He had found her!

Her whole body stilled – all senses alert and poised. Suddenly, there was a different noise. A rustle. A scrape. As if he were brushing himself against the side of the cabin.

And then everything happened at once.

The dogs broke into a volley of barking.

There was a snap of something breaking.

Followed by the most ferocious roar.

More barking and growling.

As the others woke up with a gasp, she couldn't wait any longer. She just *couldn't*. April yanked open the door and immediately a blast of freezing-cold air whipped straight into her face. She blinked once, twice, but couldn't see anything apart from a thick flurry of snow and the frantic movements of the dogs who were pulling against their leashes. Amidst the noise and the chaos, there was something else too.

Something large and formidable that was running straight at her.

'BEAR!'

Her eyes grew wide. There was a quick, fleeting glimpse of dirty white fur. A brief moment where her heart soared. And then the bear came into full view with its mouth open in a snarl and too late, April realised her terrible mistake.

This was a bear.

But it wasn't *her* Bear.

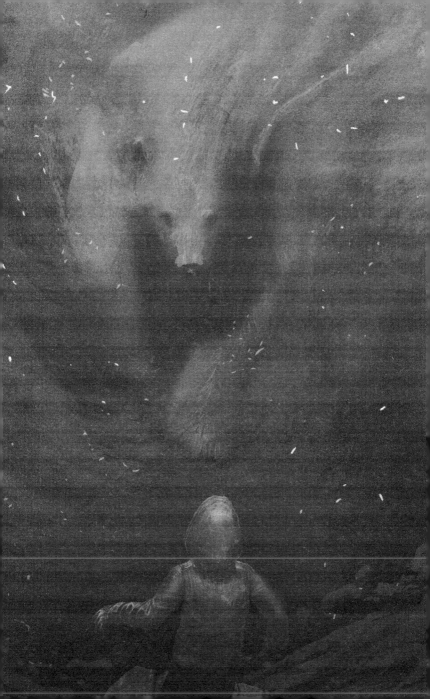

This bear was skinnier, older, more ravaged. It had pointed, yellowing teeth and all the frenzied force of something completely and utterly wild. For one heart-stopping moment the bear stared straight at her – not with warm chocolately brown eyes, but with a steely predatory stare. In some strange way it was beautiful. Even in her petrified state, April was able to acknowledge this.

But it was also completely terrifying. So terrifying she couldn't move. Her feet were frozen solid to the ground. Just as the bear was about to hurl itself towards her with a huge outstretched paw, someone grabbed her collar and yanked her out of the way.

'GET INSIDE NOW!'

Then the shot rang out.

So loud, so horrible, so shrieking that it blistered April's eardrums and made her stumble backwards into the cabin where she collapsed on to the floor.

'The bear!' she gasped. 'Don't hurt it!'

The noise of the shot had made it halt in its tracks.

April had one last look. It was an old bear. Hungry and obviously desperate. And despite the fact it had almost killed her, she felt a fierce pang of pity for it. Then Hedda shot the flare gun again, aiming into the sky with a cracking sound like thunder. The bear snarled once more before turning on its heel and running away.

Hedda slammed the door shut.

'What are you doing?' she hissed, spinning round to face April, her grey eyes flashing with anger. 'Are you trying to get yourself killed?!'

Hedda faced Dad angrily. 'I told you it was a mistake to bring her! There is a wild polar bear out there and your daughter wanted to go and say hello to it?'

She swung round to April. 'Did you not think of anyone else? Your stupidity has put us all in danger. A male polar bear like that? They are not tourist attractions. They are highly dangerous wild animals that can kill.'

'I'm sorry,' April said, sinking her face into her

hands, trying her best to avoid her father's and Tör's disappointed gazes.

'I don't care how sorry you are,' Hedda said quietly. 'We turn back in the morning.'

Chapter Sixteen

Tension

THE NEXT DAY started in silence. A silence which seemed to make the cabin shrink even further in size. On top of that, it was absolutely freezing; the sort of cold which frays tempers.

Hedda and Tör were outside seeing to the dogs – who to everyone's relief had escaped unscathed. Only some old discarded skis had been damaged. Nothing else. Inside, April stoked the fire with a poker and Dad cradled a hot cup of tea between his fingers.

Neither spoke.

It had taken all of April's persuasion to convince Hedda not to head back to Longyearbyen. Eventually, backed up by Tör, the older woman had agreed. But it was clear it was reluctantly.

April had been sure the roar was Bear's. *Convinced.* It had sounded just like him. And even at first glance, the bear had looked like him.

But it wasn't him.

The memory of the bear rearing up at her, with yellowing jagged teeth, made her shudder.

How could she have got it so wrong?

The fire in the stove was dying and April jabbed it, more forcefully this time, until it hissed and spat back. Was she really so desperate to see Bear again that she was willing to put everyone in danger?

She stabbed the fire again, banging the poker against

the iron drum so the noise echoed around the cabin.

'April. *Please*, stop doing that,' Dad snapped. 'Unsurprisingly, I have the most dreadful of headaches this morning and that isn't helping.'

'Sorry,' she muttered.

'What on Earth were you doing last night anyway?' He looked up with bleary bloodshot eyes that were full of recrimination. 'You didn't just put yourself in danger – you put *all* of our lives at risk.'

April's insides prickled. The last thing she needed right now was someone reminding her how irresponsible she'd been. Especially when she knew full well she was in the wrong.

'I am fully supportive of you and your desire to find the b . . . Bear,' Dad said, squinting at her as he removed his glasses to clean them. 'But *not* at the expense of anyone's safety – especially yours.'

'I wasn't in danger!' April answered, knowing that she was stretching the truth. 'Not *that* much anyway.'

'Only because Hedda acted quickly!' he said, replacing

his glasses and looking at her steadily. 'After returning home from Bear Island, I promised myself I would never let you get into danger ever again. And now look. Two days in and you almost got yourself killed. Maybe Hedda was right. Maybe we should turn back. This place . . . this place is far more dangerous than I had ever imagined.'

'We can't turn back now!' April cried. 'Not when we're so close!'

Dad gave a pensive glance towards the doorway, where outside the wintry embrace of the Arctic awaited them. 'Today,' he said in a firm voice, 'we will see what happens. But if we experience any more . . . encounters . . . then I'm afraid I will have no other choice but to do what is right.'

With that, he squared his shoulders.

'I knew this would happen!' April said in frustration, dropping the poker on the floor with a loud clang. 'I knew you would change your mind! It's not like you even wanted to come in the first place.'

'That's not true, April,' Dad said quietly.

'It is!' she retorted. 'It's only because of Tör you're here at all. You didn't want to come. You can't even say Bear's name properly!'

Dad let out a heavy sigh and avoided her gaze.

'See! You don't care about him!' she cried, knowing she was shouting but unable to stop the words pouring out. 'You don't care about Bear and you don't even care about me! Not since you've met Maria anyway! All you want to do is spend time with her!'

Dad looked up in surprise, a hurt expression creasing his brow. April clamped a hand over her mouth. Where had those words come from? Were they even *true*? Her heart was such a messy, confused cauldron that she could no longer tell. Either way, it was too late to take them back.

'I'm sorry,' she whispered. 'I . . . '

She was unable to say more because the door was flung open and Hedda entered. 'We need to get going. Edmund, help me load the packs. Tör can feed and look after the dogs. And you,' Hedda said, shooting April a dark look, 'you stay here.'

Dad left the cabin without a backward glance.

Even once the cabin was cleared, the dogs were harnessed and sleds loaded, he still didn't look at her. Instead, he took his position behind Hedda and April climbed wearily up behind Tör.

'It was an easy mistake to make,' Tör said, patting her shoulder.

At first April thought he was talking about her words with Dad, but then realised he was talking about last night.

'We humans are funny. When we want something so much, we end up telling ourselves anything for it to be true.'

April nodded. She was too tired to respond. Not only that, she was afraid if she did she would burst into tears. Tör hadn't noticed anyway. He was too focused on keeping the dogs under control.

At least today they would reach Sabine Land, April

consoled herself. And that meant, hopefully, they would be one step closer to finding Bear.

'MUSH!' Tör yelled. And with that, they set off.

Chapter Seventeen

Disaster

The itinerary was to travel to Sabine Land, have lunch and then turn back the way they'd come, spending another night in the hunter's cabin before returning to Longyearbyen.

The further into the wilderness they travelled, the more April's senses continued to sharpen. As if they had been lying dormant all this time and it was now only the cold Arctic air that was awakening them. Either that, or she was remembering how to be more bear.

Hedda had explained that Sabine Land covered a vast area, most of it made up of glaciers, mountains and jagged coastline. So it wasn't like April was naive enough to expect to see hundreds of polar bears just sitting around waiting for her. Polar bears were mostly solitary animals and to see just one in the wild was a privilege few would ever experience.

On arrival, even though there wasn't a single bear in sight, it was breathtaking. Under the early afternoon sun, the snow seemed to glow. Hedda had called the dogs to rest at the base of a gigantic mountain and pointed upwards where a frozen river of ice curled its way down the sides and carved out its own channel.

'A valley glacier,' murmured Dad in awe.

Hedda nodded. 'It's been here for thousands of years.' She then indicated the mountain opposite. 'You asked about how Svalbard is changing? See over there. Once upon a time, there was a valley glacier there too. Now there is nothing but a plaque to mark the spot where it used to be.'

April stifled a gasp. She knew that the glaciers were melting but not *that* fast.

'We will set up camp then have a short exploration of the area.' Hedda looked purposely at April. 'But one thing is clear. No one is to go off wandering by themselves.'

With the emergency pack on her back, flare gun in holster and rifle slung over her back, Hedda guided everyone closer to the glacier. No one was allowed to walk on it since they didn't have crampons to attach to the bottom of their snow boots and Hedda said it would be too dangerous. Instead, she kept them a careful distance away, looking around her at all times as if on guard. She seemed even more uncommunicative than usual and kept glancing pensively at the sky – not that April could see anything different about it.

Whilst everyone, including Dad, seemed to find the

glacier utterly fascinating, April couldn't help looking around with increasing desperation. Where was Bear? Was he here? Was he close? If so, why didn't he appear? It wasn't as if she could just wander off or let out a little roar either.

Mid-lunch, April purposely brought the peanut butter out of her bag and unscrewed the lid. Surely Bear would come now? Especially if he sensed his favourite food. She was just in the process of slathering some on to an oat biscuit when Hedda stood abruptly.

'We are to turn back.'

'*What?*' April gasped.

'The weather.' Hedda pointed to the horizon and April followed her gaze. It seemed a little hazier than usual, but nothing alarming. 'The forecast didn't show a snowstorm but it seems the Arctic has different plans. If we leave now, we can reach the cabin before it hits us.'

'But . . . we can't!' April cried, feeling the oat biscuit crumble in her hands. 'We've only just got here and—'

'We will still camp in the cabin tonight and it may

even be that we see the northern lights later, once the storm has passed,' Hedda replied.

April gazed at her blankly. What was she going on about the lights for? She didn't care about the lights! She cared about Bear.

'Dad!' April turned to her father but once again he avoided eye contact as he had been doing all day. No doubt he was happy they were turning around. April looked at the jar of peanut butter then back to the horizon. She smelled the change in the air, as if it had thickened, even though she still couldn't see anything.

'You tried your best, April.' Tör patted her shoulder gently. 'But we can't stay out here. Not when it's dangerous.'

'But I can't leave him!' April cried. 'Not when we're so close. *I can't!*'

'We are not leaving anyone behind,' Hedda said, hurriedly collecting the dog bowls, food containers and water bottles and packing them up on to the sled. 'We are all to leave, each and every one of us.'

April turned from Hedda to Tör, and then her father before realising she was outnumbered.

'I'll stay!' she said desperately. 'I'll stay here until the storm passes!'

Hedda shot her a scornful look. 'Don't be ridiculous. Do you have any idea how long an Arctic storm can last? Days, weeks. It is not like where you come from. This is the edge of the world and the edge of the world is not always kind. I said my word was final on this expedition and my word is that we are to leave now.'

April could feel the storm now. It wasn't just the drop in temperature. It was the difference in tone. As if the whole vibration of the Arctic had shifted an octave lower.

'We need to go,' Hedda said, clipping the last of the harnesses in place. 'Quickly!'

The huskies snapped and yelped, picking up on the invisible currents in the air. Even Hedda was struggling to keep them under control. Soon, everyone apart from April had taken their place on the sleds.

How could she leave?

How could she leave Bear when she was so close? How could she leave not knowing if he was injured or even still alive? She felt short of breath, as if a chasm had opened up and carved her in two.

'Come on, April,' Dad said, giving her a non-negotiable look. 'We have to go. *Now*.'

One leaden foot after another, she finally took her position behind Tör on the sled. In front of her, the dogs strained against their harnesses.

'MUSH!' Tör yelled.

They took off. Sliding away from the glacier. Away from Sabine Land. Away from Bear. And as they did, April felt something inside her heart break into a thousand pieces. It wasn't just that she was leaving the Arctic.

She was leaving Bear before she had even found him.

The sky was darkening and she was dimly aware of the rising wind, but it was only when Bo stumbled momentarily that she realised Tör was struggling to keep the sled under control.

'Dammit!' he swore.

The dogs returned to their shape, albeit more ragged than before, and the sled continued slowly. Ahead of the lead dog, Finnegan, April could just about make out Hedda and Dad's sled. The wind had risen sharply and it was taking all of Tör's strength just to keep them on track.

The dogs sprinted onwards.

Then a sudden clap of thunder split the skies.

Spooked by the noise, one of the dogs panicked and leaped into the air. Finnegan pulled forward, but the rest of the dogs had somehow got their harnesses tangled up. Before long, the huskies lost shape and ended up in one jumbled mess in the snow.

Tör swore again. Then he jumped off the sled, grabbing the emergency pack. 'I'm going to have to untangle the leads!' he yelled. 'Hold on to the brake tight!'

By now, snow had started to fall. Lightly at first, but quickly turning into thick flakes which whipped sideways in the wind. Ahead, Hedda and Dad's sled had disappeared into the distance, the sound of the gale masking the fact that they had inadvertently left the other sled behind.

'The reins are completely knotted,' Tör yelled. 'Can you pass me the knife? It's not in the pack!'

The knife must be in the bag of kitchen provisions just behind her. Which meant April had to loosen one foot on the brake to reach it. If she was careful she could just about do it. She stretched out.

BOOM.

Another clap of thunder punctured the air. This one so loud and frightening it made her lose her footing.

The dogs, sensing there was no one in control, burst into life. April grappled with the steering and tried to put all her weight back on the brake.

'STOP!' she cried desperately. 'STOP!'

'April?' Tör shouted. 'APRIL!'

His words were distant and muffled. The blizzard was distorting sound, so she couldn't even tell which direction they were coming from. She tried to turn the dogs around, but despite the tangled leads they just kept sprinting and sprinting until Tör's voice grew fainter.

And then it grew fainter still.

And fainter.

Until it disappeared altogether.

Chapter Eighteen

Arctic Storm

THE SNOW WAS falling so thick and fast that it took all of April's concentration just to hold on. Time became nothing but a blur. It was impossible to see or hear anything. Her goggles were clouded, all the exposed parts of her face were raw and her fingers and toes completely numb. Even with all her winter clothes on, she was still no match for an Arctic storm.

After what felt like an eternity, although she had no way to measure it, the dogs stopped, panting and heaving with their exertion.

The snow was dense, so absolute, she couldn't even see her hands or feet. It was not so much a blizzard – more of a wall. Something solid and impenetrable. April wiped her snow goggles, only for them to coat up almost immediately.

'DAD!' she cried. 'TÖR!'

But it was no use. No matter how loud she shouted, her voice kept being snatched away by the wind. A howling screech that pushed and buffeted her from all directions.

Now they had stopped moving, she could feel the cold seep into every pore of her body. What had Hedda said to do in case they got separated? Think, April. *Think.* Her brain was so dulled. Of course! The emergency pack. Thank goodness. It would have everything she needed until rescue. April reached behind her but with a small cry of terror, remembered Tör had taken it just before the dogs ran off.

Since Hedda's was the lead sled, she carried most of the provisions with her. April had a box of kitchen equipment, two boxes of dog food plus the food bowls. Apart from her own bag, which contained her sleeping bag, spare clothing, diary and some leftover cheese and rye bread from lunch, there was little else of value.

She swallowed hard.

The wind was relentless, battering her from all angles, the harsh sound of it burrowing into her head and drowning out all thoughts except one.

Hedda was right.

The Arctic wasn't a place for children. It wasn't even a place for *humans*.

April had made so many errors since coming here. One foolish decision after another. Now she was just tired. She was tired of everything. As the wind shrieked and the blizzard fell, it was oh so tempting just to close her eyes.

To shut out all the noise.

She rested her cheek against the surface of the sled. Letting the snow drift down on her flake by flake by flake. Bit by bit, the snow covered her until she lay invisible, under the surface of the world. Like that she stayed. Part of the snow. Part of the Arctic. Part of the storm. Part of nature itself.

And it was so cold, she could have slept. She *wanted* to sleep.

Until under her cheek, the Earth murmured.

At first, she thought she was imagining it.

Surely out here, the heart of the Earth was frozen?

But the heart of the Earth is never frozen. It is sometimes quiet, but it is never silent.

The Earth murmured again and something deep inside April's heart thawed and murmured back.

Not just a murmur.

But a growl.

Enough to make her prise open her eyes, blink the snow away from her lashes and wipe the slush from her face.

Hedda was wrong. She wasn't just a child. Or even a girl. She was half-bear and she would fight to do the right thing. Even if she never saw Bear again, she would still fight for him.

She would fight until her dying breath.

She would fight.

And then April opened her mouth and roared.

She roared for everything that had happened since coming back from Bear Island. And everything that hadn't happened. She roared for the warming temperatures. The hot baking summers. The rising oceans. All the animals that were dying. Most of all, the people who still weren't acting fast enough.

She roared for herself too, because what is a roar without a little bit of your own pain? Your own frustration? Your own anger.

With the roar, April clawed herself back to her feet.

As if sensing her fire, the dogs rose to their feet too.

It was then April remembered something else. Hadn't Hedda said it was the dogs who led the way? The dogs who knew where every cabin was? The dogs who could find their way to safety blindfolded?

April yelled with all her heart. She had work to do.

'MUSH!'

Chapter Nineteen

Trapper's Cabin

Letting the dogs lead was a gamble as April had no idea where they were headed. She was so cold she was operating on autopilot. But it was too late now. She just had to trust the huskies. Even though her clothes felt flimsy against the storm, she was still grateful for her fleece-lined rainbow snow boots and thick, winter jacket. Even so, it took all her strength just to hold on.

It wasn't a journey measured by time.

It was measured by the simple act of surviving.

As the skies started to darken the dogs slowed, before coming to a stop. It was still snowing hard, so at first April didn't see anything and began to panic. But then, as she wiped her goggles and peered closer, she could make out a rough outline of a ramshackle trapper's cabin.

So old it no longer even looked in use. But it was shelter.

It was safety.

Grabbing her bag, she slid off the sled, murmuring her thanks to the dogs. Then she took a step. Her foot sank into the snow and it took all her strength to yank it out. Head bowed. Another step. Then another. Her legs were so frozen and heavy that she sank to all fours like a polar bear. Like this, she crawled the last remaining metres where she shovelled the snow away from the door with her gloves as the wind lashed against her face.

But finally she was in.

It was a dark interior smelling of wood, fire smoke and kerosene. There was a bed in the corner made of broken planks, as well as an ancient, decrepit-looking stove and a wall full of rusty tools and cooking equipment. All April wanted to do was lie down and sleep. But she knew she couldn't. It was far too cold for that. Even with the door shut, the wind was howling so hard against the cabin, she was afraid the roof would blow off.

First, she had to see the dogs were okay and fed. She gave a hug to each and every one, saving special hugs for the silver-furred Finnegan, the lead husky who had taken her to safety. Once this was done, she had to get warm, so she changed out of her wet snowsuit and into dry clothes. Thank goodness she at least had her own backpack.

The thermometer showed minus twenty degrees. With deep relief, April found the stove was already full of fuel, whilst on the floor next to it was a box of matches. With numb, shaking fingers, she struck a match. For one horrible moment, she thought the stove wasn't going to ignite.

'Please light, oh *please,*' she muttered with a rising sob.

Whoosh, the flame took off.

With the fire roaring, April didn't even have the strength to make it to the bed. Instead, she lay her sleeping bag down on the hard floor and curled up in it.

All night, the storm battered and raged. As if the whole world was twisting and turning on itself. The pots and pans on the wall rattled and moaned and clanged. In the end, it was hard to distinguish one noise from another. As if Earth had opened her mouth and let out a huge, angry roar of disappointment and rage.

Something had changed. April sat up, her heart racing, her mouth dry. Somehow, she had managed to fall asleep. But now? There was no roaring or thundering or booming. Instead, there was a deadly quiet. No storm, no wind, no life. Just a vast solemn silence and a feeling of panic in her belly.

In the end it was very practical matters which drove her out of her sleeping bag. She was cold and she was hungry. The fire had died down so she loaded it back up and then ate the leftover cheese and rye bread plus a square of her chocolate and a couple of peanuts.

With warmth and food now inside her, April felt her brain whir into action. Surely, Tör would be fine? After all he had the emergency pack and would have been able to alert Hedda and her father to his whereabouts. Not only that, Hedda would have realised they had left the other sled behind and come back to find him. Hopefully they would all be together and safe.

But what about *April*?

Would they be able to find her? Would she be able to find them? Dad would be worried sick. Oh, Dad! Her tummy twisted. April hadn't meant what she'd said about Maria. Not deep down.

And now she had inadvertently done the exact thing she swore she wouldn't. She had disappeared. Again. But at least she had the dogs.

That's when she realised she hadn't heard them yapping since last night.

'Oh no!'

Getting out of the cabin was easier said than done. On opening the door she was greeted by a wall of solid snow as high as she was and it took her several minutes just to dig her way out.

She knew straight away.

The dogs had gone.

She'd been so tired and cold, she'd failed to tie them up properly.

Every single one of Hedda's rules, April had now broken.

'Finnegan?' she called hopelessly. 'Bo? Coco?'

But this time, April truly was alone.

And yet, somehow, standing in the doorway, she was too distracted by the scene in front of her to feel afraid. Before her, stretched out a new world. The shack was next to an ice-covered fjord which glistened and sparkled. Of yesterday's valley glacier there was no sign.

Behind her stood a snow-covered mountain, and in front, mile upon endless mile stretched out disappearing into nothingness. It was so empty, so bare, but also so pure that it made April feel like she'd stepped into a photograph.

But it was the skies that made the breath catch in her throat.

Emerald greens and blues swept across the sky like the most astonishing fireworks. Fingers of colour reached down from the heavens, touched the Earth and then pirouetted away, twirling this way and that like dancing figurines in the sky.

The northern lights.

Aurora borealis.

It was the most beautiful thing April had ever seen. As if she were no longer part of this Earth but had woken up in a dream world made of colours which she didn't even know existed.

And the noise! She didn't think the lights could make music. Yet it seemed fitting that such a sky could sing. It was like violins strumming against her soul.

April shuddered with the truth.

It wasn't the sky.

The sky couldn't speak.

There was only one thing which could make *that* noise.

In the distance, loping out of the horizon, he finally appeared.

'BEAR!'

CHAPTER TWENTY

Bear

THIS TIME THERE was no mistake.

He stood at a distance. His nose twitching and quivering in the still winter air and it was all April could do to stop herself gasping out loud. It was Bear. It really was *him*. As if to prove it, he rose up on his two hind legs, rearing into the sky like the brilliant white stallion he was. And as he did, the lights shone down from the sky on to his fur so his whole being shone and sparkled and dazzled.

April pressed a hand to her heart in an attempt to steady it. '*Bear?*'

Bear slowly dropped to all fours. He cocked his head and gazed around him, his ears poised and alert as if trying to tune in to what was happening.

'It's *me*,' she whispered. 'It's April.'

Maybe he didn't recognise her. She swallowed down the lump of disappointment. She hadn't changed much but she was a tiny bit taller, her face had grown thinner and her hair was more scraggly. Perhaps Vincent at the Polar Institute was right. Perhaps it was too much to ask that a wild polar bear would remember her.

'Bear?' she whispered once more.

He looked around again, from the ice-covered fjord to the endless Arctic tundra which crackled and sighed under the weight of the gleaming skies, until eventually his gaze swept full circle and came to rest on her. For one endless moment, bear and girl stared at one another.

April held her breath.

Her nerve endings thrummed, her throat felt thick and her fingers were curled up into tight fists. A kaleidoscope of emotions swept through her until she felt dizzy with them. She shivered in the cold morning air and bit her lip anxiously. Bear's nose twitched once more. He lowered his head. Then he raised it and looked at her again.

Straight in the eye.

He took a tentative step forward at the exact moment that April stepped forward. All she could hear was the soft crunch of her boots on the snow and the noise of her heart hammering against her chest.

She took another step.

As did he.

April could smell him now. Feral and musky. Wilder than before. But also a smell which reminded her of home. A smell of pure comfort.

Another step.

Now only a few metres away, she could see the soft dark chocolate of his eyes, which were pinned on her in a steady, gentle gaze. It was only then that her lip started to tremble. For they were the exact same eyes. Full of trust and love and something else. Something she hadn't seen in the longest of times.

'Bear?'

April took another step. More hurried now. More urgent. Somewhere in the far distance glaciers crackled and moaned. Dogs yapped and people searched for her. But in that moment, none of it mattered. All that mattered was right in front of her.

Bear took a step.

Then another.

Each step bigger and bolder than the last.

Each step more hurried and urgent.

Until finally they were face to face.

Under the sheen of the flickering lights, the luminous green glinted off Bear's fur and radiated out of him. April clamped her hands over her mouth.

'Oh my,' she murmured. 'It really is you.'

It was like someone had raked a comb down her back. Or plucked each individual beat of her heart. Or even doused her with the radiance of a thousand suns.

The feeling was so bright, so luminous, so pure that April felt a shift somewhere in the deepest chambers of her soul. Something that had been torn into a million pieces had now been sewn back together.

She felt complete.

Not in the sense that anyone else should ever make you feel whole. But in the sense that the universe had righted itself on its axis and all was now as it should be.

He was more dazzling than she ever could have remembered. Far more beautiful than the photograph she had gazed at a trillion times, far more magnificent than any of her memories.

He was real. He was solid. He was alive.

And he was here.

CHAPTER TWENTY-ONE

Together Again

APRIL HELD HERSELF as motionless as a statue. She was so close now, she could reach out her hand and touch Bear. But she didn't. Not because she didn't *want* to, but because she was afraid.

Not afraid of Bear hurting her.

There was never any doubt in April's mind about that.

It was a fear of the moment.

Between them was just one metre, but also seventeen months in time. In that time a lot of things had happened. She was not the same April. And gazing at Bear, she realised he was not the same Bear.

There was a graze on his rear flank, where some dried blood clung to his fur.

'That must have been where the gun got you,' April murmured, once again instinctively wanting to touch him but not daring to. 'At least it doesn't look serious.'

With a rush of relief, the fear that she might never see him again, the fear she had carried with her ever since she first heard about the shooting, dissolved and disappeared back through her feet and into the snow.

Apart from that mark, there was also a scar on his left shoulder which hadn't been there before. Not a large one, but a mark that nevertheless signified their time apart. He seemed bigger somehow, if that was possible. He had grown not necessarily in stature, though he did seem broader across the chest, but in how he carried himself.

He held his head higher, his chest more pronounced and his chin more assured.

'You're a grown-up now, aren't you, Bear?'

And for some reason, April started to cry.

Not noisy, loud sobs. They didn't belong in the still beauty of the Arctic. But the quiet, unbidden tears of someone who is feeling too many emotions at once and so this is the only way for them to come out.

As April held her hands to her face, it was Bear who reached out.

He leaned his head forward, so gently she hardly noticed it at first. Not until she felt the brush of his whiskers against her cheek and she giggled in response.

'That tickles!'

But still, she didn't dare move. Not even a muscle, though the air was so cold that her fingers ached and her feet throbbed. She stood perfectly still, feeling the Earth deep below, where it too had quietened itself as if it were tuning into the scene above. Then inch by slow inch, Bear moved his head forward even more, until finally he rested his chin ever so gently upon her shoulder.

'Oh!' April said, letting out a big whoosh of breath.

And in that moment, all of the time that had passed between them folded itself up and shrank into nothing.

'Oh!' said April again and then she threw her arms around Bear's neck and she clung on and clung on. So tightly that she thought she might never be able to breathe again. That it didn't matter if she never breathed again. Because even if she swallowed the entire universe into her soul, she still would not have shone any brighter than she did now. She held on with everything within her and this time, she knew she would never ever let go again.

April wasn't sure how long they stayed like that.

Perhaps only minutes. Possibly forever. Maybe even longer than that. But time enough to remember it really was quite hard to breathe with her nose buried so deeply in polar-bear fur. She coughed and spluttered and eventually released her arms – albeit only a fraction – and lifted her face.

'I missed you,' she whispered hoarsely. 'I missed you *so, so* much.'

In return, Bear licked the tears off her face one by one, and with them all the hurt from her soul. As he did so, April realised that even though Bear might have a few extra scars and both of them had grown older, nothing had truly changed between them. Because some bonds can never change. Not really. No matter how far apart you are.

April pulled away so she could blow her nose with a hankie. She didn't want to snot over Bear. That didn't seem fair. After she had placed the hankie back in her pocket, she repositioned herself with her cheek resting against his.

Then she sighed deeply. The kind of sigh which is made of happy things – like candyfloss, sunshine and bedtime stories. They stayed like that, cheek to cheek, and it seemed the most perfect, natural thing in the whole wide universe.

Because it was.

'When I first got back, I missed you so much. You know that, don't you?' April whispered. 'I missed you in a way I didn't think I'd ever be able to miss anyone.'

With her face pressed against his fur, she could hear the beating of Bear's heart – like the steady, reassuring thump of a clock. She wished for the millionth time that Bear could speak back. And at the same time, she realised it didn't matter. Because in his silence, he gave her something far greater. He gave her the chance to simply be herself.

'Did . . . did you miss me too, Bear?'

Bear didn't answer. But then again, he didn't need to. He pulled away and shifted his head, so now they were face to face. And then he looked at her. Not a fleeting look. But a deep drink of recognition. A gaze that contained every single beat of the cosmos and more – something unfiltered and raw and pure. The kind of gaze that everyone, at least once in their lifetime, deserves to receive.

'You found me,' she said. 'Or maybe we found each

other. But the point is, you are here. I *was* right.'

April grinned. Not an arrogant grin of victory – that wasn't her style. But a grin of joy and happiness. A grin which is infectious.

'We're back together,' she said. If she wasn't mistaken, Bear seemed to be grinning too. Although it was hard to tell. He might just have been hungry.

'Oh!' she exclaimed. 'I brought something for you.'

She pulled away from Bear, ripped open her bag and started rummaging in it. Where was it? She tossed out a few items of clothing before finally finding what she was looking for right at the very bottom. A jar of peanut butter.

'For you.'

She twisted open the jar and placed it on the ground between them. That was how Bear preferred to eat – rather than out of her hand. (It was safer that way too, just in case he accidentally bit off a finger.) If only she hadn't eaten all of her oat biscuits. No matter.

She waited for Bear to gobble it all up.

Then she waited some more. But though Bear was gazing at the jar, he didn't move.

'Don't you want it?'

Bear licked his lips. He was clearly hungry. So why wasn't he eating?

'You can't have gone off it?' April screwed up her nose. 'It's the crunchy kind. You know – your favourite.'

She nudged the jar closer to him with her foot. But even though he twitched his ears and licked his lips again, still he didn't move. She could smell the peanut butter in the air – sweet and nutty and tempting. But no matter how much she waved it in front of him, Bear wouldn't eat.

'What is it, Bear? What's wrong?'

Bear had swivelled his head so he was no longer facing April but looking behind him – back towards where he had appeared. Then he snarled. It wasn't a fierce snarl – more like the noise her dad would make if April crossed the road without looking. When he would bark at her out of protection. April tried to look over

Bear's shoulder but she couldn't see anything unusual.

'*Bear?*' April asked tentatively.

Now Bear had turned round fully and was snarling again. Even though she knew he would never harm her, April shivered. The northern lights had stopped flashing across the sky, and now everything seemed colder somehow, more forbidding.

'What's wrong, Bear? Is something the matter?'

And Bear roared.

Chapter Twenty-two

Bear Ride

APRIL HAD HEARD many of Bear's roars in their time apart but these had all been in her imagination. Sometimes she even pictured him roaring when she needed an extra dose of courage – before making a speech, or on her first day of school or even when confronting someone who didn't believe in climate change. But they weren't *real* roars. They were pretend ones.

Hearing Bear's real roar again was completely different. Like comparing a running bathroom tap to the rage of the Amazon river.

The roar swept its way across the tundra, filling every crevice, every crack and every pore. April had always thought that when she met Bear again the pair of them would stand together and roar until their throats were hoarse and their hearts full. But she sensed this wasn't a roar of greeting.

'Bear, what is it?' she asked again. 'What's wrong?'

He was gazing at her imploringly. April knew that look. It was the exact same look he'd worn the day he wanted to show her his mountain cave on Bear Island. He sank to his haunches in the snow and twitched his ears.

'You want me to get on, don't you?' she said. 'You want to take me somewhere.'

Bear blinked but didn't stand up.

April chewed her lip. She had no idea where Bear

wanted to take her or how far away it would be. Surely now the storm had passed Dad, Tör and Hedda would be searching for her. The sensible thing to do would be to stay here. The cabin was shelter – it had a stove and a stockpile of wood. There was even a possibility that Finnegan and the rest of the dogs might be able to lead Hedda and the others back to her.

Yes. This was the right thing to do.

Bear nudged her shin with his nose. When she didn't answer, he nudged her again, this time more insistently.

'Bear?' she swallowed. 'But . . . I don't know where you want to take me? I don't know if I should leave here . . . '

Her voice tailed off in the face of Bear's desperate expression. And despite everything, April knew what she had to do.

Rushing back into the cabin, she retrieved her diary from her bag. She tore out a clean page and scribbled a note to her father to let him know she was safe and with Bear.

She also took a couple of minutes to tidy the place, before packing up her things, including the jar of peanut butter, the half-eaten packet of peanuts and the remaining pieces of chocolate. There was no other food in the cabin to take with her and she could only carry what was in her backpack, though she did pack the matches, as well as a knife, with a promise to replace both later.

With one last fleeting glance at the cabin and all the safety it offered, she closed the door. Outside, she found Bear sitting on his haunches waiting for her. When he saw her approach, his eyes lit up.

'Yes, I'm still here,' she said, rubbing his nose.

It had been a long time since she had last climbed on Bear's back. But as April sank down on to his soft fur and nestled her legs around his tummy, it was like climbing back into her own bed after being on holiday. She let out a small sigh of contentment. Even though she had grown a little taller and Bear a little wider, they still somehow fitted perfectly together.

'I'm ready,' she said, patting the side of his neck.

Bear took the first few steps slowly, as if mindful April might have forgotten how to hold on. But before long, he picked up the pace and headed away from the cabin and straight across the wide flat Arctic tundra towards the white horizon. With Bear keeping her warm, April leaned forward on his back, curving into the direction of the wind and holding on to the tufts of fur by his neck.

Like this, they ran.

They ran over frozen fjords, across icy plains, and through landscape so bare and so barren that it was impossible to believe any living thing could survive here. Alongside seascapes which rose up in frozen jagged fingers, through snow that lay crisp and pure and untouched. And even though they were in the middle of nowhere and she had no idea where her father, Hedda or Tör were, it somehow didn't matter.

For the first time since arriving back in Svalbard, she felt the loosening of something inside her. A sense not just of leaving the last vestiges of civilisation but of leaving something of herself behind too. Something she had been carrying ever since she returned home from Bear Island all those months ago.

She felt the stirring of life.

The kind of alive you feel at fairgrounds, at Christmas or on the first day of the holidays that makes you want to shriek and holler and laugh all at the same time.

The feeling was so strong that she tilted her face into the sky and started laughing, big belly laughs that came from the pit of her soul and let the joy out. Then she burped for good measure, before wrapping her arms around Bear's neck.

'I'm home, Bear,' she yelled at the top of her lungs. 'I'M HOME!'

And though Bear couldn't have possibly understood, he leaped through the air as if to celebrate and April let out another laugh before gulping a mouthful of the sweet, precious Arctic air. It somehow tasted different from normal air – more vibrant, more powerful and more electric.

Still they kept on running.

They ran past a pair of Arctic foxes, scattering some white ptarmigan pecking forlornly at the ground and then through a small group of reindeer – who gazed at them curiously before returning to graze on the tough gorse hidden under the snowy plains. April wished for a brief moment they could stop. She had never seen a reindeer before. Not in the wild. But on Bear ran, until finally she could hear him panting, his breath hoarse. By now, her fingers and toes were tingling with the cold.

Eventually, after what felt like hours, Bear stopped in the shadows of a snaggle-topped mountain.

He sank to his haunches and April slid off, stiff and sore but also heart-happy.

They were at the edge of a shoreline; although in this part of the world, no waves crashed against the beach. Instead, the sea was flat and still, hidden under a thick layer of ice. In places she could see where the ice was joined together – the interconnecting caps creating a jigsaw picture. It was this frozen ice which allowed the polar bears to roam so far and so freely, hunting seals in the ice holes and feeding up for the long summer ahead.

But it was not the sea, impressive as it was, that commanded her attention.

It was the ginormous glacier towering in front of them. A blue barrier which shone like crystals. Beginning life as a large body of fallen snow, it had compacted over centuries into a solid, shifting wall of ice. She remembered what Dad had said about them being living, breathing things – as close to the heart of nature as you can possibly get.

Carved into the very centre of the glacier was an ice cave. As she stared inside, April had the strangest sensation of staring into the very womb of the Arctic.

A V-shaped entrance.

Something shadowy and hidden.

Bear padded over and then paused outside the cave before turning back to April. He tilted his head to one side and gave her a look. The kind of look which is impossible to misinterpret.

April swallowed, all her cheer evaporating in the still, sharp air. 'You want me to go in there?'

Chapter Twenty-three

The Ice Cave

Ever since April had sunk into the murky depths of the Barents Sea and nearly drowned, she had been afraid of dark spaces. And the cave looked very dark indeed – the sort of darkness which could swallow people whole and then spit out their shadows.

She gulped once more.

Next to her, Bear pawed the snow. It was apparent, even without words, that he wanted her to follow him into the cave. He nudged her shoulder just to make sure she got the message.

'It's okay, Bear,' she gulped. 'I . . . I just need a moment.'

Not that she doubted him. She trusted Bear with her life.

She just didn't know whether she *wanted* to find out what was inside. There was a look about Bear. His ears were pushed flat on his head and his nose trembled, but there was also a sense of trepidation that had not been there before. It sent an icy shiver down her spine.

'This is why you brought me here, isn't it, Bear?' April pulled her jacket tighter round her body. Now she was no longer on Bear's back, the air was biting and it whipped straight through her clothing. She reached out to lay a hand on Bear's fur for warmth. 'I'm ready.'

There were bear tracks in the entrance of the cave, but no human ones. April took a deep breath and then stepped inside.

It took a few minutes for her eyes to adjust. She had

been in a cave once at the seaside, but that had been so dark and damp, she'd scurried straight back out. But she was surprised to see that the glacier was not dark. Overhead, the arch of clear blue ice looked as though it were made of crystals, and around her the walls shimmered and glistened.

'It's beautiful,' she murmured. Part of her wanted to stop and soak it in, but she could feel Bear's breath on her back, pushing her on.

As the cave got deeper and the light from outside faded, the blues became more muted and the temperature dropped even further. April stumbled and when she righted herself, Bear had paused and become so still and quiet, he might have been a statue.

'What is it?' she whispered, something cold and clammy running down her spine.

The cave had started to taper and Bear's nose pointed towards the very end where it was dark and full of shadows. April hesitated. She didn't really want to go down there.

She laid a hand on Bear's shoulder for courage. Then she took a step forward, her eyes gradually adjusting to the darkness.

At the very end, she could see something lying on the floor.

Deep down she already knew what it was. She knew it in the depths of her soul. But she took another step anyway. Not because she wanted to, but because it was the right thing to do. And because it was what Bear wanted her to do.

In the deepest, darkest blue of the cave, where the glacier creaked and groaned and whispered, there lay a polar bear. With its eyes closed, it looked as though it were sleeping.

But April knew it was not asleep.

The bear was thin and emaciated, each rib bone clearly pronounced and the jagged bones of its hips sticking out like blades. April had seen death before. A cat by the side of the road, an elderly badger in their old back garden, the raw look of grief on her father's face.

But she had not seen death like this.

April tried to find the words but only feelings came out. A croak. A moan. A sob. Something hard and brittle.

She turned to Bear.

He was standing with his head bowed and his ears sunken. In the blue light of the cave, his eyes were dull and flat. Then the most wretched thing of all, he took a step forward and nudged the other bear's head with his nose, as if willing her to wake up.

'She was your mate, wasn't she?' she whispered. 'Oh, Bear! I'm sorry. I'm so, so sorry.'

April could stand it no longer. She flung her arms around Bear and hugged him tight. Not because it would change anything. She knew from experience of her own mother's death that nothing can do that. She did it because it showed him that she cared. That she would always be there for him. And sometimes that's all you need to hear.

At first, Bear didn't move. And as the ice crackled and creaked around them, April feared she had done the wrong thing. That perhaps he preferred to be alone with his grief – the way her father had been. But then she felt his whiskers tickle the side of her neck, and slowly Bear leaned his head into her shoulder. April lifted up her arm and curled it around him and pulled him tight.

And in that way, she took away some of his pain.

Even when the weight of his head became heavy, she didn't let go. Instead, she began to talk to him in her softest voice. 'I'm glad you found someone, Bear. I hoped you had – especially after being alone on the island all that time. I'm just sorry that it ended like this. I wish I could bring her back to life for you. If I could, I would a thousand times over.'

She couldn't know for sure how the bear had died. It might have been an illness, but she knew it wasn't.

'She starved, didn't she?' she said, pulling away so she could see his face properly.

Bear didn't answer. But April could feel the truth running through her bones, the way the meltwater had once run through this glacier and created the cave in which they were now standing.

'Oh, Bear.'

April had never felt as useless or as human as she did in that moment. It was their fault the temperatures across the planet were rising. For the average person, the fact that the sea ice was melting might not sound important. But for the animals that depended on the ice for their lives – it was everything. She wanted to shout and cry and stomp her foot in rage.

At the same time, something was niggling her. Is this why Bear had called April back to Svalbard? Because it didn't make sense. As sad and as desperate as this was, she also knew that male polar bears didn't stay with their mates – not in the way humans did. It wasn't like they didn't care. It was just that wild animals were different and polar bears more than most. For them, getting a partner was about ensuring the survival of their species. It wasn't anything to do with love or all the sentimental things humans feel. So, what did he want her to actually *do*?

Just as she was racking her brain for answers, Bear growled.

The noise was so startling that April jumped in shock.

'Bear?' As far back as she could remember, he had *never* growled at her before. Was he angry at her? Did he think it was her fault somehow? In a way, she supposed it was.

'I'm . . . I'm sorry. I'm so sorry things aren't changing fast enough,' she said, knowing that a mere apology could never ever be enough.

But Bear didn't seem angry with her. In fact, he wasn't even looking her way. With one tentative paw, he had stepped forward and now stood directly in front of the other polar bear with his head bowed and his ears twitching.

April looked at him curiously.

Then he stopped growling and made a new noise. A noise April had never heard him make before. Not a squeak, or a roar, or a grunt or a burp. But a sigh. That was the only way to describe it. The sigh a mother makes over her newborn baby. A sigh of love and wonder and awe.

April's eyes widened.

'Bear?'

He glanced back at her and in the light of the cave his eyes seemed almost blue – shining with something sparkly and iridescent.

Then he slowly stepped to one side.

And there, emerging from the hidden depths of the cave, and wobbling on four unsteady paws, was a tiny polar bear cub.

CHAPTER TWENTY-FOUR

The Cub

'Oh my!' April gasped. 'Oh, Bear!'

The cub was about the size of a puppy. Its fur was the brightest, cleanest white, and stuck out at all angles. He or she, April was unable to tell, had a smattering of snow around its muzzle and dark brown button eyes that glinted mischievously. Its face was rounder than Bear's with soft fuzzy fur. Without a doubt, it was the sweetest thing she'd ever seen.

'Well, hello there, little one,' April said gently.

She squatted, keeping a safe distance. Wild animals tended to be ultra-protective of their young and could become very dangerous if you approached them. Even if that wild animal were Bear, she still needed to be extremely cautious. Although, he didn't seem to mind her being close – perhaps because he trusted her so deeply. Nevertheless, April kept as still and as calm as possible.

After a few minutes of patient waiting, the cub became curious and emerged from its corner, sniffing the air inquisitively. It was now weaving in and out of Bear's legs playing some kind of version of peekaboo and bobbing its head out occasionally to check April was still looking. She giggled. Like all young beings, the cub overflowed with the sheer joy of life itself.

April laughed again and, caught by her laughter, the cub glanced at her with dark button eyes. On

unsteady legs, it began to totter over until it stood a hair's breadth away. Close up, she could see how white its fur was, like candyfloss. Then the cub started sniffing around her backpack, which she'd placed on the floor.

'Is *this* what you want? Are you hungry?'

Of course! That's why Bear hadn't wanted to eat the food. He was saving it for his cub.

April twisted open the jar of peanut butter and placed it on the snow between them.

'You'll like this,' she said. 'It's mine and Bear's favourite food.'

The cub looked from Bear to April to the jar and back to Bear before tottering over to the jar, sniffing it a few times and then sticking its nose right in.

'Don't get stuck!' April giggled as the cub pulled its muzzle out, peanut butter stuck to its nose and whiskers. Bear leaned down to lick it off like the father he was.

Bear had a cub?

April had done a lot of research about polar bears in the past year. One of the facts she'd learned was that cubs spend up to two years of their life with their mother, feeding on her milk for the first three months. Most male polar bears are solitary and, after mating, had very little to do with their offspring.

218

The fact that Bear, the father, was still with the cub was proof enough that something had gone terribly wrong.

The cub stuck out a pink tongue and licked its lips and April was pleased to see it seemed to enjoy it. Despite all her research she'd still not found anything about polar bears liking peanut butter, although it was claimed they had a sweet tooth. By now, the cub had finished eating and was looking sleepily around. April held out her hand, and the cub tottered over before climbing on to her lap and settling down.

'So you like peanut butter, do you?' she murmured. 'I thought you would.'

There was a blob caught on the end of its nose and she wiped it off tenderly. It was a boy cub, she realised, and he felt surprisingly light in her lap. April ran her fingers gently over his fur. She could feel the cub was thin. Too thin.

She shivered as goosebumps ran up and down her arms.

With the mother now dead, how was Bear feeding his son?

'Is that why you came to the port?' she asked. 'Is that why you were calling me? You want me to save your cub?'

And Bear opened his mouth and roared.

CHAPTER TWENTY-FIVE

A Decision

APRIL GAZED DOWN at the sleeping cub.

In her lap, he was warm and comforting. But at the same time, April felt the weight of responsibility. Like any young animal or human, polar bear cubs were incredibly fragile. In order to survive, they needed feeding regularly and preferably with their mother's milk. This was obviously no longer an option.

It wasn't like rescuing Bear before. If she had left him on the island, he might not have had a very happy life, but he would most likely have lived. This was different.

Unless she found the cub food, he would die.

And there was no way that April was going to let that happen.

What were her options?

They could return to the ramshackle trapper's cabin of last night, but not only was there no food there, she wasn't sure how to navigate her way back. It was the dogs who had guided her there, after all, not Bear.

The next option was to take the cub to Longyearbyen. But given she had no idea where she currently was, it was impossible to gauge how far away the town would be – although she had a horrible sense that they had travelled much further north. The cub might not last that long without food. Also, taking Bear to any form of human settlement carried a huge amount of danger. The last time he had been there, someone had shot him.

There was no way she could risk that happening again.

What alternatives did this leave?

Surely there would be another cabin somewhere – some other remote trapper's cabin – but how on earth would she be able to find it? They couldn't go roaming about indefinitely. Besides, with the freshly fallen snow a lot of the cabins were probably hidden unless you knew exactly where to look. Even if she did find one, the chances of it being stocked with food weren't guaranteed.

No. There had to be a better option.

She took a couple of deep breaths to calm herself. It was no use panicking just yet.

Think, April. *Think.*

She racked her brain until a tiny flame sparked in the furthest corner of her mind. Something Hedda had said. Over lunch on the second day, she'd been talking to Dad about the miners who used to live on Svalbard. April had tuned out as it was hard to understand how anyone could ravage this beautiful landscape. But what had she said?

Of course!

She had talked about various abandoned settlements. In one of them, the miners and their families had departed so abruptly they had left behind all their clothes and provisions. Surely by that same reasoning, there would be some food left in the kitchens? The mine had only closed a couple of years back. 'I wonder . . .'

Trying not to wake the cub, April reached into her backpack for her map of Svalbard. She ran her finger over the page. Until finally – there it was! Coles Bay. She remembered the name because of the irony of mining for coal.

But how far away was it?

This was much harder to calculate. Mostly because she had no real idea where she was, and even if she did know, the terrain of Svalbard all looked frighteningly the same.

However, she estimated they must still be on the east coast since they had been hugging the sealine. She ran her finger up and down the right-hand side of the map. If only she could find that snaggle-tooth-shaped mountain she had spotted just before they reached the cave. The lack of light was hurting her eyes. She was about to give up when at last, she found it.

April's tummy lurched.

She wasn't very good at reading scales on a map but, as suspected, even she could see they were a very long way from Longyearbyen. Coles Bay was thankfully closer – a thumb's width away directly west. Although how far was a thumb's width? In truth she had no idea so she crossed her fingers for luck.

'It's our only chance, Bear,' she said, hating the way her voice wavered.

She wasn't sure of the time, but sensed it was late. Right now, she would have given anything to lie down and sleep. But instead, she took off her backpack and pulled out various items until there was enough space to gently place the sleeping cub inside. Then leaving the fastening slightly loose, she put the bag over her shoulders. She kept the essentials, such as her sleeping bag, plus the items she'd picked up at the cabin. She debated whether to leave her diary but decided she could tuck that inside her jumper. But she had to leave behind some spare clothes. It was a risk to lose the few possessions she had, but hopefully she could restock in Coles Bay.

'That's you safe and warm,' she said, patting the bag. 'Now it's time to go.'

April was never fully sure if Bear understood her. Not her words anyway. Most of the time he seemed to respond to the tone in her voice – as animals do. But this time, he didn't respond even though she'd spoken quite loudly. Instead of moving closer to April, he padded over to his mate on the floor. Then he lowered his muzzle to her shoulder and nuzzled it gently.

At first, April wasn't sure what he was doing. But then realisation gently dawned.

Bear wanted to say goodbye.

Because it was a private moment and all private moments deserve respect, April turned her back. She clasped her own hands together and sent a little prayer out to the universe – not just for this bear, but for *all* the fallen bears and animals in the world, especially the ones who had been injured or killed by humankind. It wasn't like she could make up for it. But she could at least show that she cared. And sometimes caring is the best thing of all.

When she finished, she took a deep, shuddering breath and wiped her eyes with the back of her glove before turning to Bear's mate. 'I promise I'm going to do my best to save your cub.'

CHAPTER TWENTY-SIX

The Mineshaft

APRIL HAD NO way of judging how long it should take to get to Coles Bay, but after a couple of hours of riding, she was starting to doubt whether they were even heading in the right direction. There were no signposts pointing out the way. There were no recognisable markers. There was nothing but snow stretching around them in all directions.

It wasn't even like Bear Island, where she could feel reassured by the island's edges or the fact that Dad was close by. Here there were no boundaries. It was just ice and snow and mile upon mile of valley, mountain peak and fjord.

Even with Bear's comforting fur under her fingertips, when the sun started to dip from the sky, April couldn't stop her heart from skittering nervously.

They pulled up in the deepening shadow of a mountain and she slid off on to the thick snow. Using Bear's body as shelter, she gently pulled the cub from the rucksack. In the wild, cubs would feed as frequently as every three hours. A pair of dark button eyes gazed up at her imploringly.

'It's okay, little one,' she whispered as he made a strange mewing sound. 'I know you're hungry.'

Ideally, he needed his mother's milk and all the nutrients that contained. But in lieu of that, her last square of chocolate and the remainder of the peanut butter would have to do. He gobbled up the rest of the jar greedily.

Next to her, Bear's ears pricked. Somewhere in the distance April heard a low moan. A glacier? They often made strange booming noises. Or something else? Something more dangerous. April unfolded the map hurriedly.

'I just need to check where we are,' she said, squinting at it in the fading light. 'I . . . think we're heading in the right direction.'

But in truth, she had no *real* way of knowing. Each snow-ridden valley looked like the one before. Each snow-capped mountain the same. If Hedda were here she might be able to help, but then again, she doubtless wouldn't approve of April's attempt to rescue the cub. She had made it abundantly clear she believed bears belonged nowhere near humans.

The noise came again, and this time Bear rose to his feet, growling under his breath. A memory of yellowing, snarling teeth made her shiver. Was it another polar bear? Could it sense her and the cub? April knew the biggest risk to the cub was not just the lack of food, but becoming prey to other hungry bears. She quickly pulled the backpack tight, making sure he was snug and warm before climbing back on to Bear.

Under bruised twilight skies, into the night they travelled. A shadowy, frightening dark place. A place which could play tricks with your mind. Because that was the thing about the Arctic – all that space and emptiness was unnerving. Strange, unworldly noises ricocheted through the air, and one particularly loud screech almost made April fall off Bear in shock. At one point the valley they had been travelling through petered out into a dead end, so they'd had to retrace their steps. By now, April was sure they were lost and it was only the north star in the sky which gave her hope. As long as she kept that in sight, she knew they were heading the right way.

After what seemed an age, and when the cold had buried itself deep inside her skin, the silhouette of something fearful and ominous loomed on the horizon.

As they got nearer, April could see it was a structure composed of rotten wood and rusted metal, with three jagged fingers pointing up into the air like spikes.

'W-what is that?' April was so frozen, her teeth were chattering.

It was the ugliest thing she had ever seen and gave her the sensation of spiders scuttling across her skin. As they approached ever closer, slow recognition dawned.

It was a mineshaft.

In the olden days, many people were drawn to Svalbard because of the rich seam of coal hidden under its surface. This mine had obviously closed down a long time ago, but there was still something sinister about it. Something *wrong*.

Even Bear skirted it. As if he knew instinctively that somehow this thing was his enemy. Still, at least the mineshaft showed April she was close. 'We made it, Bear,' she said, relief flooding through her. 'We made it.'

There was no sign, but surely this had to be Coles Bay. Beyond the abandoned mine were about ten to fifteen ugly, uniform concrete buildings set around a square-shaped plaza. It was a bleak place. If she looked hard enough, April imagined she could see the shadows of the past floating about. She swallowed. Not that she had been expecting any sign of life, but nevertheless, she had secretly been hoping for it. For one of the buildings to be lit up with a warm, welcoming glow and someone knowledgeable and wise and kind to help her. To take the cub from her arms and tell her what to do. The way grown-ups should.

Instead, the place echoed with complete and utter abandonment.

'Never mind, Bear,' she said, trying her best to sound brave. 'We'll check the houses one by one and see what we can find.'

As Bear padded forward, she tried to dismiss the growing feeling that coming here wasn't such a great idea. Hedda had said something about extreme temperatures affecting your ability to think clearly and April shook her head as if to straighten out her thoughts.

Gigantic snowdrifts had built up against each house, making it impossible to even open a door. It would take hours to shovel away the snow.

From the bag, the cub started to mew. Little chirrups that sounded like a cross between a kitten and a puppy. In any other circumstance, it would have melted her heart. But right now, it reminded her of the urgent need to find him food.

'It's okay now,' she murmured. 'We're nearly in.'

As Bear stood guard, April circled the buildings before finding one which, because of its location at the rear, had been partially protected from the full force of the weather.

She dropped to her knees and started to scrabble at the snow with her fingertips. It was much harder than it looked since it had compacted into ice. Before long, her hands were numb and her fingers felt like they could snap off.

The cub mewed again, this time more plaintively. A horrible sound which clawed at her insides.

April swiped again at the snow but it might as well have been a block of concrete. It had been nearly two whole nights since she'd lost the others. Two nights of not sleeping properly. Two nights of not eating much. She let out a sob.

There was no way she could do this. Not *alone* anyway.

'Bear!' she yelled. 'BEAR!'

It took a few moments for him to appear and when he did, he gazed at her blankly. She had forgotten that sometimes it took him a while to understand.

'W-w-we need to get in,' she said.

She was just about to scrabble at the snow to demonstrate, when Bear launched himself shoulder-first at the door and the whole thing collapsed under his weight.

'That's one way to do it,' April said, stepping over the remnants, feeling guilty for breaking in. But then the cub yowled in hunger and she told herself to stop being so silly. No one had lived here for years and it was hardly a home any more. Besides, if she stayed outside, it wouldn't just be the cub who died.

It would be her too.

Luckily the broken outer door led into a closed inner porch, which then opened into a square-shaped room. There was no electricity, but after a few minutes fumbling in the dark, April found some candles that she lit with the matches she had taken previously. In the flickering light, she saw they were in a small, enclosed space which smelled of stale memories. There was a worn sofa and an armchair, a stairway that presumably led to a bedroom and an open doorway which revealed a galley kitchen, fitted with various cupboards and shelves. She headed there first, pulling open every door and drawer in the desperate hunt for something to eat. She found an assortment of cooking instruments, cutlery, hunting knives and even a corkscrew. But any food that had been there was long since gone.

In its place was a thick layer of dust and a smell which made her nose wrinkle.

'It's okay,' she said to herself, more for comfort than anything. 'No need to panic.'

But it was hard not to feel alarmed, especially when the cub's howls were becoming increasingly urgent.

Bear had disappeared. Presumably to do bear things and have a scout about the area and make sure they were safe.

In his absence, the house felt even more deserted. She felt as though she was the only person left on the planet. What if Bear didn't come back? What if she were trapped here forever? Oh, why had she brought them here?! Why had she thought this was a good idea? April kicked the side of the cupboard in desperation and, as she did, a solitary can rolled out from underneath where it must have been dropped and left many years ago.

She knelt down and picked it up with trembling fingers.

'Custard,' she said, wiping the dust away from the label. 'Perfect.'

Chapter Twenty-seven

A New Name

In any other circumstances, April would never have touched it. It was years out of date. But this was an emergency. She fished around in the drawer once more. Where was that can opener? She could have sworn she'd spotted one earlier. Ah. There it was.

The can was rusty and the can opener even rustier,

so it wasn't the easiest to open.

'At last!' she exclaimed when she had finally wrestled the lid off.

She gave it a sniff. It smelled okay. Admittedly, it was slightly congealed so she stirred it with a fork.

It would have to do.

April gently pulled the cub out from the rucksack and, as she did, the sound of his mewing filled the cabin.

'Food time,' she murmured, cradling him in her arm.

She tried to put his face to the can but all that happened was he got a blob of yellow custard on his nose. It looked so silly that April giggled, despite herself. His tongue tentatively licked it off. 'That's it! You can do it.'

She placed some custard on her finger and gently opening his jaws, she put the tip of her finger in the cub's mouth. She wasn't sure if the cub liked the taste as he made a funny noise. But he was so hungry that after a few seconds, he started to suck and she let out a sigh of relief. Just like Bear, his tongue felt surprisingly smooth. After feeding for a few minutes, the cub took a brief, unsteady wander around, bumping into various things before sniffing her rucksack and pawing at it.

'You can smell something, can't you?' April said, as he pressed his nose against the bag. 'What's in there?'

The cub poked his head into the bag and then reappeared with the half-eaten packet of peanuts dangling from his teeth, which he then shook from side to side before gazing back up at April with bright, hopeful button eyes.

'You need a name, don't you?' she murmured, stroking his head where it was all soft and fluffy. 'I can't just call you Baby Bear. You need your *own* name. A name that's right for you.'

Unlike with Bear, the name didn't come easily. She didn't want to call him Fluffy, Snowy or Icicle as they were all too obvious. She sat gazing at him for a flash of inspiration.

The cub, who was now licking the inside of the peanut bag, looked up as if he knew April was addressing him.

There was a stray half-peanut clinging to his whiskers.

'That's your name!' she exclaimed. 'Peanut. It's *perfect*.'

At which point, a loud gust of wind battered against the door frame. Peanut squeaked very loudly and covered both his eyes with his paws as if to protect himself from harm.

'Ssshh, Peanut, it's okay,' April whispered. 'You're safe now. You're safe with me.'

April stroked Peanut until he appeared calmer. Then he climbed gingerly on to her lap, where he curled up in a tight ball and drifted off to sleep.

They needed some proper heat. So, carefully placing Peanut in her sleeping bag, she set about tackling the stove.

'Where's the fuel?' she wondered.

Despite a thorough search, she found only a few small scraps of driftwood and an old newspaper. April picked it up out of curiosity. It was in English and the main headline was about the mine closing. Another article in the same newspaper talked about the warming temperatures and the Paris Climate Agreement pledge.

It was dated over five years ago.

She scrunched up the newspaper in her hands and was about to hurl it across the room when Bear entered. Compared to Peanut, she was struck by just how huge he was. Hard to imagine that once he had been the size of a puppy too.

Even though there was hardly any space, Bear somehow squeezed his way in, before settling down beside her on the floor with his head resting on his paws. April's heart lurched just looking at him. She had been so focused on saving Peanut, she'd almost forgotten the sheer joy at being reunited with Bear again.

She leaned in, enveloping herself in his warmth and he seemed to edge closer to her too, as if grateful for her proximity. It was like being wrapped in a blanket made of a thousand hot water bottles. Perhaps slightly pongy ones that smelled of damp fur. But warm and snug all the same.

As Peanut squeaked in his sleep and Bear gazed at her unblinkingly, April felt the weight of his hope settle on her shoulders.

'We'll stay the rest of the night here,' she said more confidently than she felt. 'And then come morning we'll search the other houses to see if there is any more food.'

There was no point mentioning what would happen if she couldn't find any. Instead, she reached out her fingertips and stroked the soft fur under Bear's left ear. Just the way he liked it.

'We'll be okay,' she whispered. 'I promise.'

Chapter Twenty-eight

A Confession

After the stove had burned out, April slept curled up against Bear. He lay on one side, April curled into his tummy and Peanut tucked in next to her. And despite everything, it was blissful.

She woke up feeling refreshed but also hungry. But Peanut was even more hungry. He had climbed from her on to Bear's tummy and was standing on four wobbly legs with his mouth wide open and mewing insistently.

'It's okay, Peanut. I'm going to find you some food.'

Peanut must have understood in some way as he squeaked so hard in excitement that he tumbled off Bear's belly and fell on to the floor with a soft plop. He tottered to his paws and looked at April indignantly as if it were her fault. Meanwhile, Bear flicked one eye open and, seeing Peanut was unharmed, closed it again and returned to his sleep.

'You've seen it all before, haven't you, Bear?' April giggled. 'That's right, leave him to me.'

First, she fed Peanut the remainder of the custard from last night, saving only the tiniest dab for herself. Then she pulled on her boots, her winter jacket, her hat and her gloves. Leaving Peanut wrapped up in her sleeping bag, she opened the door.

In the pale violet dawn light, April could get a better sense of the tiny settlement of abandoned houses. Whilst she had seen the disused mineshaft last night, she hadn't spotted the discarded pieces of rusted metal or the fact that Coles Bay was actually set against the nape of a fjord – currently frozen. But even in the clear light of day, it still felt forlorn and forgotten.

April's plan was to enter each house and see what provisions she could find. But, like last night, getting in wasn't exactly easy. Eventually, just when she thought her fingers would fall off (thank goodness for insulated gloves), Bear got the cue and started digging the snow away with his gigantic paws. By the end of her search, she had accumulated three more tins of custard, a tin of peaches in syrup, some dried packets of meat stew and, most miraculously of all – three packets of peanuts. She'd also found various other things that weren't edible but which she collected anyway. Some more driftwood. A saucepan. Some matches.

She stopped only to give Peanut his food. By now she'd worked out he needed feeding every four hours. If he wasn't fed he would let her know about it with loud squeaks and even the occasional naughty nip on her finger. Luckily it didn't hurt. Unlike Bear, he was a fussy eater and would only eat the food if April hand-fed him. Then she had to wait until he'd fallen asleep before she could feed herself. It meant that mealtimes lasted forever – not that April minded. Looking after Peanut filled her belly with a warm, fuzzy feeling. The way that the sun lights you up and makes you feel sparkly even on the gloomiest of days.

After lunch, April placed all the collected food and equipment on to the floor to get a clearer sense of how much they actually had. On the other side of the room, Peanut was playing a game of hide-and-seek with Bear's paws. Bear seemed to tolerate this until he grew impatient and picked Peanut up by the scruff of his neck and placed him on the sleeping bag as if to say *Enough*.

April looked up.

It was strange how Bear being a father didn't change any of her feelings towards him. In fact, if anything, it made her love him even more. As Peanut finally settled, curling himself up into a tight ball, Bear lay with his face on his paws, his eyelids shut.

'I'm not surprised you're tired after everything you've been through,' she said, eyeing the bloodstained graze on his hindquarters where the shot had grazed his skin. A flare of anger rose within her. How could Hedda think *bears* were the problem? It was humans who were leaving scars everywhere they went!

Placing the final items of food on to the floor, her stomach dropped. They might be all right for another night, maybe two at the most. But at some point, the provisions would run out and then what? Peanut needed food otherwise he would grow weak very quickly. And not just peanuts and custard either. He needed *proper* polar bear cub food, rich in nutrients. A rumble to her belly reminded her that she needed proper food too. She glanced anxiously over to Bear, whose chin was resting comfortably on his paws. He seemed to trust that she could naturally find a solution.

'Let's decide what we're going to do next,' she said.

He glanced up at the sound of her voice.

'We can stay here and you can try to catch us some food. Maybe some seals?' Bear looked at her as though this was the most ridiculous plan in the entire universe. 'I know I don't eat seal. I'm guessing Peanut doesn't either. Not yet anyway. So yes, let's discount that one. Besides, I'm not sure Dad will like that very much.'

Guilt ran over her. What would Dad be thinking now? Were they still looking for her? Had he thought she had died? The thoughts made her feel light-headed and not altogether pleasant, so she pushed them away.

'We can't go back to Longyearbyen. It's too far. Even getting here last night was much harder than I thought it would be.' Though the room was warm, she shivered at the memory of the long, dark journey across the alien landscape.

Not only that, Bear had let out a low growl. She wasn't sure if it was the mention of Longyearbyen or perhaps some distant danger only he was aware of. Nevertheless, she leaned forward and stroked his face with her fingers.

'I know something bad happened to you,' she whispered. 'And I know it can take a while to forget bad things. I'm the same with water. I . . . I haven't been in the sea once since I got back from Bear Island, even though we live next to the coast.' April sighed. 'Granny Apples says I just need to dive straight back in. But she doesn't get it. No one really gets it, to be honest. You know, sometimes the only people who do seem to understand are the ones you least expect. Like Maria.'

Bear looked at her questioningly.

'Oh, of course, you don't know who she is. She's Dad's new girlfriend,' April said. 'She's a teacher. She said I didn't have to go in the water until I was ready.'

She paused, toying with a loose thread on her jumper.

'Is she nice?' She nodded guiltily. 'She's very nice. She wears multicoloured scarves, bakes flapjacks made with peanut butter and has these loud jangly bracelets shaped like elephant tusks. Not real elephant tusks obviously. But she got them from Africa. She likes to travel to new places because she says it opens her heart.'

Bear regarded her with an open, honest expression. April lowered her own gaze.

'You're right. There is something I'm not telling you. It's just that . . . I wanted Dad to myself a bit longer. Is that selfish of me? He'd been missing for so long after Mum died. Not *missing* missing, but missing on the inside,' she said. 'But after we got home from Bear Island, he changed . . . he became happier. We spent time together. Just me and him! Then . . . then Maria came along.'

April dug into the deepest parts of her heart where all the ugliest emotions were buried. 'The truth is . . . the truth is I felt a bit jealous.'

Even though she was exposing the worst side of herself, as she looked up at Bear, she realised he wasn't judging her. At least, not as badly as she had judged herself.

That was the power of friendship. The power of the *best* kind of friendship.

In this brave new light, April felt the truth of

something quite important. It wasn't Maria she disliked. It wasn't even this new version of Dad. It was the fact everything was changing – even the planet underneath her feet. 'And sometimes it's so fast . . . it scares me. But when I see Dad again,' she couldn't bear to say 'if', 'I'm going to tell him that I'm happy for him. That I'm happy for *both* of them,' she said. 'Even if that means having a new mum.'

At that moment Peanut woke up, gazed around him and squeaked loudly. It was just coincidence, of course, but it was almost as if the word 'mum' had sparked something in him.

'Bear,' April said excitedly, something bright and shiny clicking into place in her head like magic. 'I think I have a plan.'

CHAPTER TWENTY-NINE

The Plan

'It might be the silliest plan ever invented. But do you remember Lisé?' April said. 'She's the one who met us off the boat when we first arrived in Longyearbyen.'

Bear yawned. Of course, he wouldn't remember. He'd only met her for seconds.

'The important thing to know is that she likes polar

bears almost as much as I do,' April continued. 'That's why she's gone to Friesland to monitor the birthing dens. What if . . . what if *we* were to go there too? We could take Peanut! We could try to find him a new mother. A polar bear mother.'

The cub, as if sensing her excitement, squeaked again – louder this time. April stroked his soft muzzle and he licked her fingers hungrily.

'The truth is, Bear – I can't keep feeding Peanut. Not forever anyway. It's not that I don't want to,' she said hurriedly. 'But he can't stay with me. He needs a *proper* mother. Not a human one, but a polar bear one. Someone who can feed him and also show him all the things polar bears need to do to survive in the wild.'

Bear shifted on his paws and studied her. In the gloomy light of the cabin, it was hard to know what he thought of her plan.

'I don't want to let him go,' April said quietly, 'if that's what you're thinking. Just like I didn't want to let *you* go either. It was the worst day of my life saying goodbye to you. After everything we had been through together. The thing is, you're grown up enough to know the difference between me and other humans. But Peanut? Peanut's still young. He's got his whole life ahead of him. If he stays with me, then he'll become too used to humans. And I don't think . . . I don't think that's a good idea. He needs to grow up and know that not all humans are kind. Not all humans will be as nice to him.'

Peanut had fallen asleep again, drifting off with his face resting in the palm of her hand. Such a tiny thing who had put all of his trust into her hands and her heart lurched at the thought of letting him go. Then her heart lurched again. This time at the thought of letting Bear go – for the second time.

'Do you know, at school, some of the other kids called me Bear Girl?' April said. 'I hated it at the time. Not because they were teasing me but because they weren't taking what I said seriously.'

Bear growled. He was so attuned to the vibration of

April's words that he could pick up on her upset.

She stretched out a hand and buried her fingers into his thick fur. It was much coarser than Peanut's but just as warm and welcoming.

'It's okay. The thing is I *was* a bit different from everyone. That's what happens when you become half-bear. You stand out a little bit. And it wasn't like I didn't try to fit in. Because I *did*,' she said. 'Dad thought starting somewhere new would help make things easier. But it didn't. It just reminded me that I'm not like other children.'

April paused. She hadn't talked about her innermost feelings for such a long time. So long, she'd almost forgotten how comforting it was to share them.

'That's why I don't want the same to happen to Peanut. It'll be too dangerous for him.'

Bear remained silent.

'Look – we're here,' April said, pulling out the map. 'And Lisé's camp is up here. In the north part of Svalbard. It's much closer than Longyearbyen. And it'll be safer for you there too. Lisé won't hurt you. I'm not saying it's going to be easy,' she said, sounding braver than she felt, 'but what other choice do we have?'

Chapter Thirty

Help Arrives

April tried to ignore the multiple flaws in her plan, especially now she was carrying Peanut and the extra food. Packing her bag, it was obvious she didn't have the space to pack everything. She would have to leave even more of her clothes and provisions behind.

Nevertheless she pushed her misgivings to one side.

She could stay here, or she could try to do something.

And doing something was always better than nothing.

Stepping outside, April had to swallow twice just to calm her nerves. If possible, the day had turned even colder, with a harsh, bitter wind blowing directly from the north. It was so strong that it took multiple efforts just to clamber on to Bear's back.

'I'm ready,' she gulped.

Because the wind was whipping in her face, April tried to crouch as low as possible, which was more difficult than it looked when you were carrying quite a large bag with a polar bear cub on your back. As they left the small settlement, April gave it one last glance. As much as this place of abandoned buildings spooked her, it was still shelter and warmth and now, once again, they were heading into the unknown.

They didn't get far.

As they were passing the mineshaft, a sudden, fierce gust of wind hit them sideways.

It was so powerful that it snapped off a chunk of the

rotten wood and sent it tumbling towards April. She ducked. Tried to grab a tuft of fur. Missed. And then slid clean off Bear's back.

'Aaarrgh!' she cried through a mouthful of snow.

Luckily Peanut seemed unscathed. But it was useless. They wouldn't be able to travel like this! She was just summoning up the strength to figure out their next step when Bear roared. A rumble that shook every bone in her body and even made the mineshaft rattle.

'What is it, Bear?'

A storm? A wild polar bear who had sniffed them out?

Just as April's hackles rose, there was a different noise. A dog whining. A bark. Another bark. Then the whoosh of blades.

'APRIL!'

She sat up. Blinked once. Twice. Then she broke out into the widest grin. She could hardly believe her eyes.

'TÖR!'

He pulled up the sled, jumped off and was about to

dash over, but one sight of Bear's snarl and he stumbled to a halt, his face turning sheet-white as Finnegan and the other huskies barked furiously.

'Bear!' April said hurriedly, relief pouring through every cell of her body. 'Look, don't you recognise him? It's Tör. He helped save you last time. He's a friend.'

Bear continued to snarl, revealing long sharp teeth and exposed gums. Even April trembled a little bit. Bear might be her best friend but it was a reminder that at heart he was truly wild. Eventually he quietened to a low growl, keeping one careful eye pinned to Tör – who gingerly stepped round him and shoved out a hand so he could help pull April to her feet.

'I'm glad to see you're safe and alive,' he said, pulling off his snow goggles to reveal blue eyes smiling with mischief.

April smiled back. She had a million and one questions but she was so happy to see Tör and the dogs that she didn't know which to ask first. In the end, she started with the most obvious. 'How did you find me?'

Seeing that Bear wasn't about to maul him to death, Tör relaxed marginally, although he indicated the pair of them should head into the mouth of the mineshaft where the wind was less noisy. Or maybe it was just to get away from Bear, who himself was keeping a wary distance from the pack of nine dogs.

'One minute I was telling you to keep your foot on the brake and the next you had just disappeared!' Tör said, frowning. 'I called your name but I couldn't see a thing in the snow. Then Hedda and your father returned.'

April's stomach tightened with guilt. 'What did he say?'

'He wanted Hedda to start a search party straight away but she was adamant that the dogs would have taken you to safety. She said we must wait out the storm otherwise we'd all end up dead. But the next morning, as we were about to head off and look for you . . . that's when the dogs returned.'

'They did find their way back!' April vowed to give them all a huge hug.

Tör nodded. 'They guided us to the cabin where you had spent the night and we found your note saying you had gone off with Bear.' He paused. 'Your father seemed certain you would go back to Longyearbyen, like you had last time. So, he insisted on heading there with Hedda. But I wasn't so sure. Your note didn't say anything about where you were going so I convinced Hedda to let me stay out and look for you.'

'And she agreed?!' April said incredulously. 'She believed I had gone off with Bear?'

'Well, not *exactly*. She agreed to me searching for you. But she thinks the Arctic has got into your head. Given you hallucinations. In her mind there is no way a girl can be friends with a wild polar bear.'

It was April's turn to growl.

'She seemed pretty upset that she didn't see the storm coming,' Tör said, quickly moving the conversation on. 'I think she felt quite responsible.'

April nodded. She could understand that.

'Anyway, I have the dogs and the sled. We can set

off for Longyearbyen straight away and let your father know you are safe.'

'Ah,' she replied, 'about that.'

'What?' Tör asked, his eyes narrowing. 'Why are you looking at me with that face?'

'I'm not going back to Longyearbyen. Not yet anyway.'

'Why?'

April knew she could trust Tör, but even so she took a deep breath. Then she pulled the backpack off her shoulders. As she opened the bag, a squeak came out. Even in the darkness of the mineshaft, she could see Tör's jaw drop open in shock.

'Is that what I think it is?'

She nodded. 'He must only be about twelve weeks old. Maybe a tiny bit older. But it's the reason why Bear wanted me here. To help. The mum . . . the mum died.' April swallowed, thinking of the emaciated female polar bear in the ice cave. 'I need to take him to safety. So he can be looked after properly.'

'You should have just left him,' Tör said.

'Then he would have died too!'

'Yes, but you can't go around picking up wild polar bears. It's dangerous, April. Do you know that other males kill cubs? It is like putting a target on your back.'

April held the bag close to her chest and gave Tör her best pleading expression. 'That's why we have to save him.'

'*We?*' Tör raised one eyebrow.

'I was going to do it alone but it would be easier to have help.'

'April Wood,' Tör said with a grimace. 'What exactly do you have in mind?'

'Do you remember the day we left? Lisé took a group of volunteers to an outpost in the far north that same day. She was planning to monitor the female polar bears during the denning season. To check the breeding and survival rates.'

Tör nodded warily.

'I'm going to take Peanut there.'

'*Peanut?*' Tör said, then shook his head. 'Why not just take him to Longyearbyen? To the Polar Institute like you did with Bear? I can take you both there direct now. It is about two days' journey, perhaps a bit longer, but we can make good speed.'

April glanced over his shoulder, where the dogs and the sled awaited. It would certainly be easier than heading once more into the unknown. But then she remembered Hedda's flare gun – when she had fired a warning shot at the polar bear. She could still see the fear and desperation in the older bear's eyes.

'No!' April said. 'I can't take Bear there. It's not safe for him in town. Besides, Peanut needs to grow up with other bears.'

'It is the most reckless plan I have ever heard!' Tör exclaimed. 'That is, after taking a boat on the Barents Sea single-handedly and trying to set sail to Svalbard. Do you know how vast and dangerous the northernmost part of Svalbard is? And you were going to head there alone? What about your father?'

April didn't answer. Instead, she held the bag even tighter to her chest and pulled her most defiant expression. 'Some things are bigger. I'm meant to do this, Tör. Don't you see? I'm meant to save Peanut. It's why Bear wanted me here in the first place. It's why he called me.'

As if tuning in to the passion of her words, Bear roared. Not a little roar. Not even a Bear-sized roar. But a roar on behalf of all the polar bears across the Arctic who needed help just to survive.

In response, Peanut poked his head out of the bag, opened his mouth and let out the tiniest of roars. Granted, it wasn't quite as loud as his father's but it was a roar all the same.

'See! Even Peanut agrees with me!'

Tör closed his eyes. When he opened them again, he settled his gaze on April.

'Then we'd better hurry.'

CHAPTER THIRTY-ONE

The Northern Lights

BEFORE THEY SET off, Tör and April briefly returned to the settlement, where they collected the clothes April had been set to leave behind. In addition, she was relieved to see all the additional food and equipment Tör had brought with him on the sled.

Before leaving, Tör wanted to check the route. Pulling

out the by now creased map, he ran his fingers along the page.

'We should be able to reach Friesland tomorrow. But first we have to cross the Widjefjord.'

April glanced to where his finger was pointed on the map.

'It's one of the widest fjords in Svalbard,' he said with a furrowed brow. 'We could go round it but that would take many more days. The quickest route is to go direct across it and hope the ice is still frozen. It should be at this time of year.'

A shadow passed across his face, but before April had time to question it, Tör thrust the satellite phone in her hand.

'We need to call your father,' he said, 'let him know you're safe.'

April took the phone with slippery hands. She had never been good on the phone at the best of times – let alone when faced with an undoubtedly furious father. Still, she needed to let him know she was safe. The satellite phone was notoriously temperamental, but after dialling his number a couple of times, it finally started to ring.

'Tör! Any news?' Hearing her father, April's insides crumpled at the sheer exhaustion evident in his voice. 'Hello? Hello?'

'It's not Tör,' she said quietly. 'It's me. It's April.'

'*April!*' Dad said in a tone she'd not heard for a long time. It was relief mixed with fear and for a second April felt a sharp pang of homesickness for him – for his aniseed candy and tousled hair. 'Oh thank God, you're safe!'

She nodded. Then realised he wouldn't be able to see her. 'Yes,' she said. 'I'm fine.'

'B-b-but where are you? What happened?! Where have you been?' Dad's questions tumbled out so thick and fast, they left April dizzy.

'I'm at Coles Bay,' she said, and then gave a very brief explanation of how she'd ended up there and why. By the time she'd finished there was such a long silence on the other end of the line she didn't know if the phone was still working. 'Can you hear me?'

'Yes,' he said slowly. 'I can . . . but I'm having trouble taking it in. Do you know how worried I've been? I've been so afraid at the thought of you out there all alone! And now you want to go *where*?'

Saying it out loud did sound a bit silly – even to her own ears. Maybe it would be better if she returned to Longyearbyen? At least then, Dad could help. But then she caught a glimpse of Tör checking the sleds, the wagging tails of the dogs and finally, Bear, who was patiently waiting for her.

'To Friesland,' she said, straightening her shoulders. 'To save Peanut.'

Dad ranted and raved for a few good minutes, but given he was so far away, there was nothing he could do to stop her. In the end, she was saved by the line. It started to crackle and break up so much she couldn't even hear him.

'I can't . . . you're . . . this!' he said, his voice tight with fear.

'I'm sorry, Dad,' she whispered, aware that she was

breaking the promise she had made him. 'I . . . I love you.'

The signal died and she put the phone down shakily, taking a moment to compose herself. Then with a forced smile, she gave a thumbs up to Tör, who was harnessing the dogs. No point telling him that Dad wasn't quite as on board as she had hoped.

'Who are you riding with?' Tör called out.

Up until this point, Bear had been keeping a distance. It wasn't Tör's fault. And nothing he was doing wrong. Only that Bear had been born a wild animal, and most wild animals don't necessarily trust humans, especially of the non-April variety.

April looked from the sled to Bear, and back to the sled again.

It made sense to go with Tör. The sled was relatively comfortable, it was certainly warmer and undoubtedly far less dangerous. She knew she could trust Finnegan and the other dogs. It would be the sensible option.

'I'm going with Bear,' she announced.

'I thought you would say that. You two are inseparable.'

'*Three*,' April answered. 'We three now.'

Tör rolled his eyes, but not unkindly. Then he took his position on the sled. April – with Peanut tucked warmly in her backpack – mounted Bear.

And finally, with Bear and April leading the way, they set off.

The first hour or so was uneventful. Using Tör's GPS, the unlikely convoy travelled north over miles of untouched, pristine snow and under skies that were billowing. After a couple of hours, they stopped for a snack. As Tör tended to the dogs, April fed Peanut. Worryingly, he didn't appear hungry and seemed listless. Maybe even lighter in weight? The sooner they got to Lisé's camp the better.

After a couple more hours of speeding north under darkening skies, they stopped for the night and set up their tent. After tending to the dogs, Tör made sure to put all the safety processes in place. On top of that, they had Bear keeping guard.

April sat by the small fire with Peanut resting on her lap. This far north, the sky was so alive, so dazzling, it was like looking up into the heart of the cosmos. So many stars it was like a trillion different universes all at once.

'The world is so beautiful,' she murmured because there was a sense of awe and hush at breathing it in. 'I don't get why people won't take better care of it.'

Tör was gently stroking Peanut's soft fur. A small smile crept on to his lips as the cub lifted up his chin, before settling it weakly back down.

April shook her head. 'Sometimes I think . . . I think it would be better if I didn't care so much.'

Tör raised a questioning eyebrow.

'You didn't see the bear in the ice cave. She had starved to death! And that's because of *us*. Because of what we've done to the planet. When I lie awake at night, sometimes that's all I can think about. Not just the bears. But *all* the animals all over the world who are suffering.'

'That's not your fault!'

'But what have I really done to make a difference?' April said. 'I thought it would be easy. I thought I would go home and tell people and then they would just *do* something. But they're not doing anything and now we're in exactly the same place – only worse!'

'It's not fair that we're the ones who are going to have to deal with it. It's not fair that the world is changing,' Tör said matter-of-factly. 'But that doesn't mean we don't try.'

'But *how*?'

'The human race is like the husky pack,' Tör said, indicating the slumbering dogs a few metres away with Finnegan, the lead dog, in their centre. 'It needs leaders. People to look up to. People to follow. You're *that* person April.'

'You make it sound easy,' she replied. 'So why aren't they listening?'

'Because you scare them,' Tör said quietly, so as not

to wake Peanut, who had fallen asleep. 'They're scared by someone standing up for what they believe in. Most people don't stand up for their beliefs. They just find it easier to bully someone who does.'

April nodded. She knew this to be true, but it didn't make it any easier to deal with.

'You know my dreams, April?' he said. 'My dreams are to make the local football team, get a job which pays well and maybe one day get my father to accept me for who I truly am.'

'They're lovely dreams!'

'But *your* dreams, April. *You* dream of saving the world. That's what makes you different. That's what makes you extraordinary.'

'I don't feel extraordinary,' she said in a small voice.

'You might not be the tallest, or have the loudest voice, but you lead with your heart. And that's the best way to lead. It's the *only* way to lead,' he said. 'A real leader has the courage to speak up for change even if other people disagree.'

April sighed in gratitude for her friend. Tör always knew how to make things feel better.

'Anyone can be a leader,' he said simply, 'if they decide to be.'

April felt both the vibration of his words but also the movement of the stars overhead, as if they too were dialling in. As she gazed up, the sky started to shift and dance. Not just with stars but with fingers of dazzling emerald light pirouetting across the sky.

As she breathed, she realised something both profound and simple at the same time.

She was not just a child.

She was made of the stars, the light, the very breath of the universe.

And the universe shines bright within us all.

CHAPTER THIRTY-TWO

The Fjord

COME DAWN, THE huskies set their noses towards the scent of the north. As they travelled, the landscape became ever more stark and barren. This close to the North Pole was a place of nothingness and yet in that nothingness, there existed all the beauty of the planet in its purest form.

The majestic shape of the mountains silhouetted against violet skies, the golden glow of the sun rising slowly on the horizon so it shone like butter against the ice. It was beyond the edge of the world – beyond the edge of anything April had ever experienced in her life. It was so huge and so colossal that it stole the breath from her throat and layer by layer, stripped away all the parts that had ever made her doubt herself.

For hours neither Tör nor April spoke.

Late morning they stopped to feed Peanut. He was now only picking at his food and appeared withdrawn, repeatedly hiding his eyes with his paws and trying to curl up into a tight ball.

'There's something not right,' April said worriedly. 'Look, he's not even licking the food off my hand like he usually does.'

Tör nodded. He had been distracted all morning. 'What is it?' she asked. 'Is it Bear?'

Whilst the dogs were tied up, Bear was prowling in the distance as if keeping guard. 'I'm not sure I'll ever get used to Bear. But no. It's not that.' He hesitated. 'It's the fjord. I said it should be frozen this time of year but . . .'

'But *what*?'

'Just something Hedda said, do you remember? How some of the fjords which used to be frozen solid in winter don't even freeze any more.'

Something in April's expression must have stiffened, because Tör offered her a quick reassuring smile. 'We just have to pray it is.'

Nevertheless, as he climbed back on the sled and she remounted Bear, she couldn't shake the tightness in her belly.

It took just over an hour to finally reach the edge of mighty Widjefjord. An hour where April hoped and prayed the ice would be frozen enough for them to cross safely.

April and Bear arrived first. She slid off his back, keeping one hand on his shoulder as they gazed across to the other side. It was the brightest part of the day and the light of the snow and the ice were so powerful that she had to blink a few times so her eyes could adjust. Even then, the horizon seemed to stretch on forever, disappearing into a milky far-off distance.

It was a very long way to the other side.

In the crisp northern breeze, Bear's nose quivered.

'What do you smell, Bear? Do you smell the camp?'

Tör pulled up on the sled, the dogs barking and yapping, but as always keeping a wary distance from Bear. 'What is it?'

'I think he can smell we're nearly there,' April answered. She pulled off her backpack and checked on Peanut, who didn't even let out a squeak when she opened the bag like he usually did.

Tör took a look at the fjord and frowned. 'The ice . . . ' his voice petered out. 'The ice looks *wrong*. This time of year it should be so thick you could drive a tractor on it. But see how it is breaking up over there?'

April looked to where he was pointing. To her it all looked the same. But then she noticed how the colour of that part of the ice was different. More of a bluish haze.

'It's what Hedda said,' April said as Tör tested the edges of the ice with the blunt end of the pickaxe. 'Do you think it's safe to cross?'

'I think so – if we tread carefully. But it's a risk. We . . . we could go the long way.'

April shook her head. If they went the long way, it could take days. Days that Peanut probably did not have. She wasn't a doctor or a vet. But she was wise enough to know time was running out.

'Okay, Bear. We're going to need your help.'

She remembered the last time she had proposed a plan to him – to take the boat and travel to Svalbard – and how Bear had roared in anger until she had forced him to change his mind. Back then she had been scared. Although not in any real sense. How could she be? She'd had no clue at the size of the dangers ahead.

This time she was all too aware. She knew what lay beneath the ice. She knew how dark and cold and bottomless the water was. And yet, if she showed any of her fear to Bear, there would be no way he'd cross the fjord with her on his back.

'We're going to have to trust you,' she said in her calmest voice, gazing deep into his eyes as Tör looked on. 'You lead the way and Tör will follow.'

All polar bears had huge paws. By spreading their weight evenly, it's how they navigated the ice. In this way, Bear could easily distribute his weight so as not to fall in. And hopefully pick out the safest route.

April climbed on to Bear's back, checked Peanut was safely in the bag and then crossed her fingers. The first step was tentative and the air whistled through her teeth, as the ice creaked and groaned under their weight. But it held firm. The next step was just as cautious. And then the next.

Behind her, she could hear the slice of the sled's blades and the breathing of the dogs. Then there was an ominous sound of cracking and a sharp yelp.

'The sled is too heavy!' Tör yelled.

April coaxed Bear to a gentle halt. Behind her, Tör's

normally calm face was ashen.

'What about if we take some of the things out?' she called back. 'It'll make the sled lighter.'

After removing a few items, they tried again. But whilst Bear could pick his steps, with the combined weight of the sled, its provisions and Tör, the dogs did not fare as easily.

'Be very careful!' She held up a hand to warn Tör.

The huskies gingerly took a few more steps before grinding to a halt. Tör was trying to urge the dogs on, but April could see that his hands were shaking.

They were within touching distance, but it felt like miles.

'It's not safe for you,' she said, shaking her head.

'I can try a different way!' Tör cried, scanning the ice desperately.

'No.' April bit back her fear. 'I think . . . I think you need to turn back. It's too dangerous.'

Then she smiled at her friend. Not your average smile. But a smile that reassured him that she would be all right. A smile that gave him permission.

In the face of that smile, all Tör could do was nod reluctantly. 'I'll go the long way,' he said at last.

'Yes,' April said, putting on her bravest face. 'I'll see you there.'

There were a million and one other things April wanted to say. But as she watched Tör turn round and reach the safety of the shore, none of them seemed to come out.

'April Wood!' Tör yelled over his shoulder. 'Be careful!'

Then he turned to wave once more, just a small figure now, before disappearing off into the distance.

'It's just me and you now,' she murmured to Bear, pushing her shoulders back for courage. 'And Peanut.'

She gazed ahead at the wide, seemingly never-ending fjord. But there was no time to panic. Peanut hadn't made any noise in ages. Not even to mew for food.

'Just take it nice and easy, Bear,' she whispered, climbing back on to him. 'Nice and easy.'

With her heart hammering in her chest, she clung on to Bear's fur as he carefully picked his way across the ice, until April estimated they surely must be halfway because here the ice was at its thinnest yet. It had a faint translucent feel and even the smell was different – something weak and watery. Under Bear's weight, the ice splintered and groaned, providing just the most fragile of barriers to the dark icy water. Just as Bear was taking another cautious step, she heard the desperate yapping of the dogs behind her.

Tör?

Why had he come back? Had he somehow found a way safely across?

She glanced behind her hopefully.

With a thud to the chest, she quickly realised it wasn't Tör.

It was Hedda.

Chapter Thirty-three

On Thin Ice

For a split second, April could do nothing but stare at her. Dad must have told Hedda where they were headed. But how had she got here so quickly?

Beneath her, Bear stirred. As if sensing there was more danger than just the brittle ice.

'She won't hurt you,' April said. 'Not with me on your back.'

Yet as she looked behind her once more, she spotted something she hadn't seen first time round. A flare gun. And just as she spotted it, Hedda lifted one hand off the sled and fired it into the air.

It was louder than thunder. Bear leaped forward in shock, almost dislodging April head-first on to the ice. 'Whoa there! It's okay.'

She gripped hold of his fur, hoped Peanut was safe, and then looked behind her again. The sled had gained distance and was now close enough so April could see the set expression on Hedda's face, the way her felt coat flapped behind her and the unmistakable outline of a rifle over her shoulder. In Hedda's mind a polar bear meant just one thing – a threat to human life. The flare gun was meant to frighten. To make a bear back off. But if that didn't work, then she would resort to using the rifle.

With a horrible, sickening clarity, April remembered what Hedda had said about shooting to kill – how they aimed at the heart. 'No!' she cried.

She slid off Bear's back, trying her best to ignore the creaks of the ice underfoot. She grabbed Bear's face, his muzzle, a tuft of fur, anything. 'You have to go!'

But Bear was an animal. And animals don't always do your bidding. Instead of leaving, he nudged April's shoulder. How could he leave? How could he *ever* leave?

'I know you want to protect me,' she said, quickly taking off the backpack and placing it next to her feet, so she could hug him properly. 'I know you love me, but you have to go. *Please*, Bear!'

Bear stood there. His whiskers trembled and April could sense his fear. Bear wasn't afraid of many things. But he was afraid of humans carrying guns. Behind her, she could hear the blades of the sled swishing closer along with the hard panting of the dogs. She didn't dare look.

'I promise I'll look after Peanut,' April said, her voice breaking. 'I'll take him to Lisé and I'll make sure he finds a new mum. I'll do what you wanted me to do. But go. Go for your own safety.'

April dropped her hand from Bear's fur. Rubbed her face. Then did something she never thought she would ever do. She slapped Bear's rump and she raised her voice to the one animal in the world she loved more than her life.

'GO!'

Still Bear was confused. April slapped him again. Bear cocked his head and twitched one ear.

'Go!' she sobbed. 'Please just *go.*'

Bear took one last puzzled look at her and started to back away. As he did, April stood alone on the ice.

Watching, watching, watching as Bear walked away. Slowly at first. Then faster. Until he was running across the ice of the fjord, each paw step leaving cracks in her heart. But at least he was safe.

'Goodbye, Bear,' April whispered. 'Goodbye, my love.'

The sled was so near now she could smell the musky scent of the dogs. The smoke from the flare gun. Even the sweat from Hedda.

April cautiously turned round. As she did, the ice made a strange eerie noise. Something like fingers on a chalkboard. Menacing and unworldly. Hedda had brought the dogs to a stop mere metres away.

'DO NOT MOVE!' Hedda cried, a panicked look on her face.

'Hedda?' April asked.

There was a massive screech, a loud scraping and a lone panicked bark.

Followed by the unmistakable sound of breaking ice crumpling under April's feet.

The break was so sudden that she didn't even have time to grasp on to the edges of the ice. One minute she was standing there, and the next she had dropped straight down into the water.

The shock was so fierce it took her breath clean away.

She burst to the surface. Tried to grab something but it was no use. The edges were too soft to hold on to properly. But she reached for them anyway. Flailing with her hands. And then her fingertips.

Even in the midst of blind panic, April knew she had only minutes, if that, before the cold temperatures killed her. Then she would slip under and disappear into the dark depths forever.

Even as every part of her body started to numb, she was relieved Peanut was safe. The bag thankfully hadn't fallen into the water with her.

At least one of them would survive.

She reached for the edge of the ice once more. Her hands moving slower and more sluggishly now.

'Stay calm!' Hedda's face appeared above her. 'Grab hold of the rope.'

The rope was just there.

April stretched for it. But her fingers were so numb they couldn't hold on. She clasped it, Hedda yanked.

But it was no use. April fell back into the water. Hedda swung the rope again.

'Try to hold on!'

Somewhere above, someone was shouting her name.

But it was cold.

So bitterly cold.

April closed her eyes.

The water settled around her like frost.

And then it all . . .

. . . went . . .

. . . black.

Chapter Thirty-four

The Rescue

. . . but in the blackness was something else.

Something that was swimming desperately towards her. Something remarkably familiar. And someone who would never ever just leave April to die. Even in her semi-conscious state, she was aware of the huge jaws gently closing around her body, the sensation of being taken back to the surface.

The water streamed from her as she was placed on to the safe ice, and then as she lay shivering he licked her face. Once, twice, then again for good measure.

'B-B-Bear!' she whispered.

And then she passed out.

'April?' The voice was distant. 'April?'

She slowly opened her eyes. She was lying on a mountain of fleeces and furs on the sled, with new warm clothes, a thermal blanket and what seemed to be the entire team of huskies lying on top of her.

April spluttered. There was some dog fur up her nose and it was tickly.

'Thank goodness. You're awake,' Hedda said, leaning over her and placing a cup of steaming hot chocolate to her lips. 'Drink this.'

'W-w-where am I?' April asked. Her mind was hazy, full of ice and fog and cold. She took a sip and her insides exploded in warmth.

'On the north side of the fjord,' Hedda replied. 'I didn't want to risk staying out on the ice any longer.'

April nodded, sinking her head back down into the fleeces. Then she gasped. 'Bear!'

A strange look passed over Hedda's face. One that April didn't like. 'No!' she whispered. 'Please say you didn't!'

Hedda shook her head. And then pointed to some distance away where Bear stood with his head poised, waiting.

April let out a small gasp of relief. And then she started to cry. Not just from the relief at seeing him. But at everything that had just happened. Her body was still shuddering from the effects of the cold. Her mind desperately trying to catch up. She had fallen into the icy water. She had nearly died.

Hedda narrowed her eyes thoughtfully. 'It was an unbelievably foolish thing to do. But he saved your life.'

'Of course he did!' April said. Then tried to sit up, which was hard with thirteen dogs resting on you. 'Just like your dogs would rescue you if you were in trouble!'

Hedda encouraged April to stay lying down. 'Keep your energy,' she said. She seemed about to say something else, then changed her mind. Instead, she gently stroked the head of her lead dog, Ripley.

'When you went missing, your father told me about you and the . . . the bear and how that was the real reason for the trip,' she said. 'I didn't believe it. Not even when I saw the note you had left. I thought you had lost your mind. The Arctic does that, you know? It seemed too . . . too preposterous to be true. An animal like that simply cannot be friends with a young child.'

'Well, it is true,' April said crossly, feeling the life slowly creeping back into her body. 'He's too scared to come closer. But he won't hurt us.'

'I can see that now.'

April wanted to roar. To let Bear know she was safe. But she was too weak. Instead, she sneezed. There was still dog fur up her nose. This sneeze was quite loud. Loud enough to dispel all the last bits of fog from her brain.

'PEANUT!' She sat up with a gasp. 'WHERE IS HE?'

'Peanut?' Hedda looked at her as if she really were hallucinating.

'MY BAG!' April yelled. 'WHERE IS MY BAG?!'

Would Hedda have left it on the ice? Please no! It wouldn't be fair. Not now they'd got this close. She grappled around her, trying to find it.

'This bag you mean?' Hedda said, reaching out to grab it from behind her. 'It is quite heavy. What do you have inside?'

'I'll show you,' April said, taking the bag and hoping against hope Peanut was all right. She opened it, then softly pulled the cub out. He was limp, barely breathing but he was miraculously still alive.

'This is Peanut,' said April.

Hedda shut her eyes for the longest of times. Had April pushed Hedda too far? Finally, she opened them. Eyes the colour of storms and wolves.

'Well, hello, little one. You look like you need some help.'

Chapter Thirty-five

Lisé

Hedda found some special sugary feed she kept on the sled in case any of the huskies got hurt or injured. 'It gives them a lift,' she explained.

April watched as she tenderly fed Peanut through a syringe, her whole face softening in the presence of the tiny cub. Peanut mewed. Which was positive. At least he was making a noise. At least he was alive. Hopefully, the feed would give him enough strength for the final part of the journey. In the distance, Bear looked on approvingly. At least, she hoped so. She hoped Bear understood that Hedda was no longer a threat.

'You don't really hate polar bears then?'

Hedda barked in laughter as Peanut lay curled up in her arms. 'Does it look like it?'

April looked at her questioningly. 'What about the poor bear outside the cabin?'

'The only reason I nearly shot him was because he was seconds away from killing you,' Hedda said bluntly. 'The bears have many enemies but I am not one of them.'

She was just like Svalbard, April decided. Beneath her harsh, forbidding exterior, there was something really quite warm about her.

'But . . . but everything you said about keeping bears and humans apart?'

'You have seen for yourself how Svalbard is changing,' Hedda sighed. 'Even this ice. Ten years ago it would never have been so thin. The less ice there is, the hungrier the bears become, and the hungrier they are, the more unpredictable their behaviour.'

'That's why we need to do what we can to try and protect them!'

'I fear it is too late,' Hedda said quietly. 'The more they seek out human habitat the more risk there is. Not just to humans. But to the bears themselves. Not everyone is as kind as you, April.'

'Not *everyone* needs to be as kind. Just enough people,' April said. 'Because if there are enough people, then surely those in power will have no choice but to listen. We don't want *their* future. We want our future! A world where animals and humans can live side by side safely.'

'The dreams of youth,' said Hedda. 'I had forgotten how shiny they are. But there are dreams and there are impossible dreams. Where would you even start?'

April lifted her chin. 'We start by saving this cub.'

After explaining her plan, Hedda insisted that April rest whilst she prepared for the journey. She was also insistent that April continue by sled for safety's sake. Hedda knew where the camp was and seemed confident they would reach it within a couple of hours. The only risk was whether Peanut would make it. He had perked up after the feed but was still weak and listless. To keep him warm, they had put him inside a special thermal-lined carry case that Hedda used to keep food warm. She punched some holes in the top so he could breathe and then wrapped the case in a blanket before resting it on the foot of the sled.

'We must make haste,' Hedda said, after harnessing the dogs.

April shook her head. 'I need to speak to Bear first.'

Hedda opened her mouth to protest but then nodded.

Bear, who had been keeping a distance, pricked his ears as April picked her way carefully over to him. Her legs still felt weak so it took a lot of effort.

'Bear?' she said softly. 'You know I didn't mean what I said back then on the ice. I was just . . . trying to protect you.'

Bear lowered his head. She hoped he understood. Just in case he hadn't, she laid a gentle hand on his neck. 'I haven't said thank you yet. You saved me. You saved my life again. And now I'm going to do my best to save Peanut's life.'

Behind her, she could hear the dogs yelping in excitement, impatient to go.

'I'm going to ride with Hedda but you . . . you can follow if you want? Then when we get to the camp that means you can stay at a safe distance rather than coming in. But I understand if you don't want to come any further.' She gulped. 'It's up to you.'

Bear stared at her impassively. Then he lowered himself to his haunches and let out a low murmur of indignation. April grinned and hugged his neck tightly.

'April!' Hedda called. 'It is time to go.'

April kissed Bear quickly on his nose, before returning to the sled and wrapping herself up in a warm fleece.

'MUSH!' Hedda cried. And they were off.

It wasn't long before April spotted the tiniest of dots in the distance. It took a while before those dots transformed into canvas tents. The closer they got, April could see there were six sturdy, industrial-looking white tents, some the size of a small cabin with square roofs and zipped-up doors. Dotted around the site were pieces of professional weather-measuring equipment that reminded April of Bear Island.

As the sled zipped forward, April craned her neck to check behind her.

As she suspected, Bear had ground to a halt a safe distance away. 'It's okay, Bear,' she called out. 'I'll see you soon.'

No doubt he would go off and do polar-bear things, but April was sure he wouldn't leave until he knew Peanut was safe. She waved goodbye as the sled sped the final couple of hundred metres into the camp before pulling up outside one of the canvas tents.

Underfoot, the snow was well-trodden and there was a faint smell of cooking in the air. But even though the huskies had announced their arrival with a flurry of barks and yelps, no one came out to greet them.

'Perhaps they've left already?' April bit her lip anxiously.

Just then, there was a loud unzipping of one of the tents and out stepped a young woman with purple hair and rainbow boots.

'*April?*' Lisé stepped forward, astonished. 'What are you doing here?'

Up until this moment, April hadn't quite believed she'd ever make it. Now she was here, she didn't know what to say.

'It's a long story,' Hedda said, stepping forward. 'I'm Hedda, by the way.'

'Pleased to meet you.' Lisé stuck out a hand, before turning back to April and gazing at her incredulously.

Still, April struggled to find her voice. It was impossible to capture everything she had been through. So she stepped off the sled, lifted the carry case over to Lisé and opened it.

Lisé's eyes widened and if April wasn't mistaken, Hedda seemed to be enjoying the reaction.

'We didn't know where else to take him,' April said. 'His mother died . . . and Bear brought me here to rescue him.'

Lisé looked around her. 'Bear is here too?'

'Not in camp,' April said. 'We didn't . . . didn't think it

was safe if he got too close. But that's the reason why I came back to Svalbard. Because Bear called me. He called me because he wanted me to save his cub.'

Being told that a polar bear had somehow beckoned a human halfway across the world might have sounded a bit far-fetched to most people. But Lisé merely nodded.

'Nothing fails to surprise me with you, April,' she said with a kind smile, and then switched her attention to the carry case. She peered inside and frowned.

'I . . . I couldn't just leave him.'

'You did the right thing. Not necessarily in the right way, but every bear is precious, particularly the younger ones.'

Lisé carried the case into one of the larger tents, and April and Hedda followed. Inside, it was set up like a science lab with various research instruments occupying the space. Lifting Peanut carefully out of the carry case, Lisé placed him on a table where she felt around his tummy, inspected his mouth and finally weighed him. 'He's extremely malnourished and very light for his age. You said you found him?'

April filled Lisé in on what had happened, her voice breaking as she got to the part about the mother bear.

'I'm not sure why she left her den but it is likely she was disturbed by human activity or perhaps was forced to leave early because of hunger.' Lisé picked Peanut up gently. 'There is simply not as much food as there used to be. That is why we do the research we do. To see how the birthing population is changing and what we can do to halt the decline. Anyway, it is a miracle this one has survived.'

'Not a miracle,' Hedda said, placing a hand on April's shoulder, 'just determination.'

'Will he live?' April asked, her eyes fixed on Peanut's.

'We will try to do everything we can,' Lisé said, then wrinkled her brow thoughtfully. 'There is a female actually. She had two cubs but lost one of them about a week or so ago. Normally when a mother loses her second cub it's because she isn't strong enough, but this wasn't the case. We could try to see if she will accept this one.'

Hedda nodded. 'I have done this many times with pups whose mothers have rejected them. It can work very effectively.'

'It is a risk, of course,' Lisé replied. 'She might reject him and in doing so harm him. But in the circumstances, it is the best and most natural option.'

'A new mum,' April breathed, hardly able to believe her plan might actually work. 'Did you hear that Peanut?'

And Peanut squeaked.

Chapter Thirty-six

Unexpected Arrivals

THE PLAN WAS to introduce Peanut to his new mother as soon as possible, but it was important he was strong enough first. In the meantime, April and Hedda were invited to stay in one of the tents, sharing with another of the scientists based in camp. There were four accommodation structures in total, housing eight scientists, plus the larger-sized laboratory tent and then a shared community space where everyone gathered to eat.

There was limited space in their tent, so whilst Hedda unpacked the sled, taking only what they needed, there was one very important thing for April to do – phone her father. She dialled his number on the camp satellite phone.

'Strange. No one is answering.'

She tried calling multiple times throughout the rest of the day and even tried Jurgen's hotel. Still nothing. After whispering goodnight to Bear and letting him know about the new plan – it wasn't safe to leave the camp but she knew he would hear her anyway – she retreated to her tent. But all the time, she couldn't stop the gnawing in her tummy. Why wasn't Dad answering? What if something had happened to him?

She'd only just managed to fall into a troubled sleep when she was woken by a cacophony of loud and frenzied barking. In the gloomy light, Hedda was already up and dressed. April swiftly followed, stumbling out of the tent and blinking under the light of a million stars.

Her attention was diverted by another bout of barking and then the distinctive shape of a sled pulling into camp. As members of the research team came and went at all hours of the day, only a couple of curious scientists poked their heads out of their respective tents to see who was arriving at this hour.

April's heart skipped a beat.

'It's Tör,' she said excitedly to Hedda. 'He's made it!'

As the sled came to a halt, she noticed Tör wasn't alone. There was someone standing on the sled behind him. Someone remarkably familiar who had taken off his snow goggles and was peering around anxiously.

'Dad?'

April let out a wild cry of recognition as she hurled herself into his arms before he barely even had time to step off the sled. He smelled of aniseed candy, of something warm and familiar. Most of all, he smelled of Dad.

'You're here!' she said, hiccupping against his chest.

'Of course I'm here,' he murmured. 'And not just me either.'

It was then April noticed that another sled had pulled up, and that two more people had arrived and were standing alongside Tör and Hedda. April looked. Rubbed her eyes. Then looked again.

There was Jurgen, wearing the deerstalker hat which covered his ears, and a pocket watch clipped to the outside of his snowsuit, but also looking the most animated she had ever seen him.

And next to him, wearing a red and white spotted scarf, was Maria. She looked bone-shatteringly cold but the magic of the Arctic was clear on her face.

April disentangled herself from her father's arms, walked straight up to Maria, then gave her a huge hug.

For the next couple of hours, the three of them caught up in the warmth of the community tent. It turned out that when Dad had arrived back at Longyearbyen after the storm, and realised April hadn't returned as expected, Maria had insisted on joining Dad in Svalbard.

'I . . . I couldn't have coped without her,' Dad said,

holding both Maria's and April's hands. 'Not after you went missing again.'

'I'm sorry, Dad,' April said, squeezing his fingers. The worry of nearly losing her was etched over his face and she wished she could smooth it all away.

It was Maria who leaned over, straightened his glasses and tucked a lock of stray hair behind his ear. They shared a small smile. Not a smile that made April feel left out. But a smile which made her feel content. Because if the Arctic had taught her anything, it was the power of love.

How it is never finite.

But how it can grow into something far bigger. Big enough to change worlds.

And to change you too.

'I've told Maria all about Bear,' Dad said, clearing his throat. 'And why we came to Svalbard to look for him.'

'I always suspected there was more to the story,' Maria replied, turning her gaze to April. 'Then again, I always suspected there was more to you.'

It was April's turn to explain what had happened since the snowstorm. It was quite a long story to share so Dad made some hot chocolate, served with an emergency ration of marshmallows, and Tör, Hedda and Jurgen joined them.

As April recounted her adventure, she arrived at the part where she had crossed the fjord and almost died. With a secret glance towards Hedda, she quickly skipped over that section. There was, after all, a limit to what Dad could handle in one sitting.

'You survived a snowstorm, a night in an abandoned mining town and you still managed to bring Peanut here in one piece!' Maria said, her eyes sparkling, whilst Dad looked on with a mixture of pride and horror.

'A true soul of the Arctic,' Hedda said, patting April's shoulder. 'I don't know anyone else, child or adult, who could have done this.'

'I just did what I had to do,' April replied, blushing. 'Peanut needed me. The Arctic needed me.'

She paused. Since being reunited with everyone,

she had been so full of relief and excitement that she hadn't stopped to think about what would happen next. Now a niggly feeling of unease crept into her belly. For the arrival of her family also signalled an ending. The moment when they would have to go home and she'd be forced to say goodbye to Bear and leave all this behind again.

'But it's not over yet,' she said, gamely turning her attention back to the room. 'The hardest part is yet to come. We need to settle Peanut with his new polar bear mum and . . . hope she will accept him.'

'And that he accepts her,' Maria said, offering a shy look at April.

'I'm sure he will,' April replied, smiling shyly back.

'How long will this process take?' Jurgen asked, looking at his timepiece.

'Lisé said Peanut will need a couple of days to gain strength. Then she'll introduce him back into the wild,' April replied. 'Please say we can wait until we know Peanut is safe. Please, Dad!'

'Well, I hadn't much thought beyond finding you but since we've only just arrived . . . ' He shrugged. 'What does everyone else think?'

'Svetlana would never forgive me if I left now!' Jurgen exclaimed. 'I am happy to stay.'

'Me too,' said Tör.

'There is no question. We stay,' Maria said. 'Chester is with your mother and I hear keeping her very good company. It turns out he loves apple pie.'

The five of them turned to Hedda. She gazed back with her eyes the colour of storms.

'Miss out on the best bit?' Hedda said. 'Of course I will stay.'

Chapter Thirty-seven

A New Dawn

I<small>T WAS STILL</small> dark but the camp hummed with quiet activity as Lisé finished packing the snowmobile with one very important piece of cargo.

Peanut.

In the three days since April brought him to camp, he'd been fed on a regular diet of milk supplement and had filled out and regained most of his strength. Sat in the middle of his wire cage with his black nose pressed up against the edge, he let out a series of indignant squeaks. Her heart gave a little leap as it was the first time she'd seen him since leaving him with Lisé.

She'd been advised not to visit him so that the bond between animal and human could lessen. This was to give the cub as much chance as possible to be accepted by a new mother – although the chances of rejection were still high.

The six of them, plus Lisé and another scientist, set off early on separate solar-powered snowmobiles. The only absence was Bear. April had had one brief faraway glimpse of him since they had parted ways at the edge of camp, but she had nevertheless been keeping him updated about Peanut's progress. The only sad thing was as Peanut got stronger, it meant she was one day closer to saying goodbye to Bear again.

But she tried not to think about that too hard.

The dens were situated further east, nearer the coast.

Along the way, Lisé explained how maternity dens were dug into snowbanks, where the female bear carved out an oval room with an entrance tunnel leading in. Because of the insulating qualities of snow, the heat given off by a bear would keep the inside of the den warm and snug even when outside temperatures were below freezing.

After a couple of hours' ride, Lisé brought them to a gentle halt. In the far distance April could see the ocean stretching out in a field of ice.

'This is the nearest we can get safely,' Lisé said quietly, indicating for everyone to crouch down low. 'The wind is blowing from the east but if we get any closer, then the mother will smell us and be panicked.'

'Where is the den?' April whispered.

In the growing light, Lisé pointed to the base of a mountain about 200 metres away where a plateau of snow had built up in the leeside of a steep overhang.

'The snow there is at its deepest, and ideal for creating a den,' Lisé explained. 'Unlike other bears, the polar bear does not hibernate. Instead, she lowers her body temperature by a degree or two, which helps reduce her energy needs.'

'Which is how she can survive for as long as five months without food!' April answered.

'That is true,' Lisé said. 'Which is why the biggest challenge for the female polar bear is to accumulate enough fat on her body before denning, especially now that the ice-free periods are longer than before.'

Hedda nodded thoughtfully. Jurgen was busy taking photographs to send to Svetlana, whilst Tör and Dad were helping the other scientist with some temperature measuring equipment and Maria had rolled up her sleeves and was busy seeing what she could do to help. To April's surprise, despite the cold, Maria had fallen in love with the Arctic, saying it was the most beautiful place she'd ever been.

Lisé nodded to April.

It was time.

April crouched down so she was face height with Peanut. 'It's goodbye, little one.' Peanut, as if understanding something important was happening, pressed his paws to the edges of the cage and poked his nose through. 'I don't really like goodbyes, to be honest. But . . . I just wanted to say how glad I am that we met. I didn't think it was possible to love anyone as much as I love Bear. But you showed me how to open my heart even more.'

She placed her fingers next to the cage and Peanut licked them.

'Thank you, Peanut,' she whispered.

April took a deep, shuddering breath and nodded back to Lisé, who picked up the cage and indicated that everyone wait quietly. April positioned herself on the snow, sandwiched between Tör and Hedda. The other scientist kept guard with a flare gun just in case.

She watched through binoculars as Lisé walked cautiously, pausing every couple of steps before continuing, until she reached the base of the snow drift. It was there she opened the cage. April gasped as Peanut's face popped out.

As Lisé calmly retreated to a safe distance, Peanut tentatively made his way out of the cage, standing on the fresh snow and sniffing the air curiously as if he could smell a new beginning. Against the bare, sweeping landscape, he looked tiny.

It was only as the first rays of sunshine started to pour over the horizon that April was able to make out the disturbed patch of snow which indicated the entrance tunnel about fifty or so metres from Peanut.

'The den,' she murmured quietly.

Not that it looked like a den. There was only a small entrance visible. April kept her eyes peeled for any signs of life. It would be the mother who would come out, drawn by the smell of a cub, although Lisé had explained any potential union might not even happen today.

Peanut gazed around him again at the endless horizons.

Then the snow around the entrance to the den moved. Out emerged a black nose. An inquisitive pair of eyes. Huge padding paws. The bear gazed about her, her snout twitching. She directed her gaze towards Peanut, who seemed to shiver in the breeze.

Next to April, Hedda let out a sharp exhale of breath.

On unsteady legs, Peanut took a step closer to the den.

The mother waited at the den entrance. Half in, half out.

Then she stepped forward. Leaning her head towards the cub.

April stifled a gasp.

As if sensing something, Peanut scampered forward, slipping and sliding on the snow until he stood only metres away. The bear took another step. And another. Until she was standing right next to him.

Then with the sun casting golden waves on to the snow, the mother leaned forward, licked Peanut from head to paw and invited him into her life.

Chapter Thirty-eight

Goodbye

'Well, Bear,' April said. 'It's time.'

They were standing on the outskirts of camp. Somewhere behind her were her father, Maria, Tör, Jurgen and Hedda. The sleds were prepared and the dogs harnessed in readiness to go back to Longyearbyen.

Her heart quickened and she could feel that Bear's

heart quickened too. She squared his face in her hands so they were gazing at each other. His chocolate eyes twinkled, melted and poured into her own. 'We've been through a few adventures together, haven't we? But Peanut is safe now. And it's time for you to be safe too.'

Bear nudged her shoulder and she wrapped her arms around him.

April tightened her grip, kissed him a thousand times and then kissed him a thousand more. Time rushed, sped up and shortened, racing as fast as her heart. Behind her the dogs barked impatiently.

Then April smiled. The smile of someone who has a very big and very delicious secret. She even let out a small giggle.

'It's not goodbye,' she whispered, raising her gaze and looking Bear straight in his eyes. 'Not *this* time.'

Bear cocked his head and looked puzzled.

'It's a see you soon,' she confided, her tummy flipping in excitement.

There was no way that Bear could have understood, but something in the tone of her voice made his eyes light up and his ears waggle.

'Because this is where I belong,' she said, her heart soaring. 'With you.'

And with that, April lifted up her head and roared.

Epilogue

Home

April sat at her new desk, the one nearest the window on the back row. There were only a few children in the class. Some had been born here, but most, like her, had come from faraway places all over the world. There were so many different nationalities that she couldn't even count them on the fingers of both hands.

The teacher entered the room and took a kindly look around, before settling her gaze on April. 'Welcome to Longyearbyen school,' she said. 'The northernmost primary school in the whole of the world. I bid you a warm welcome. And what is your name?'

Before answering, April looked out of the window. It was why she had chosen this seat after all. It gave her a panoramic view of the fjord and the mountain pass beyond. Although she couldn't see Bear she knew he was somewhere out there.

He would *always* be there for as long as she lived here.

And she was going to live here a long, long time.

In the end, the decision to remain in Svalbard hadn't even been April's idea. It was Dad's. The evening before they were due to return to Longyearbyen, he had sat April down and asked her what she thought about staying. At first April thought he meant staying a few extra days in camp. But he shook his head. He meant stay, actually *stay* in Svalbard so she could finish her schooling here. April didn't need to answer. She'd just thrown her arms around his neck and clung on.

There were not enough words in any human language to say thank you.

April had been a bit worried at how Dad would cope living here, but he said as long as he got a regular stash of aniseed candy he would be fine. But then Maria had tapped him quite forcefully on the shoulder and Dad had cleared his throat, hummed and hawed, before shyly admitting he had asked Maria to join them here too.

April couldn't think of anything more magical. Deep down she secretly hoped they might even get married one day, as long as she could be bridesmaid and still wear her rainbow snow boots.

After returning to Longyearbyen, everything had happened quickly. Within days, Dad and Maria had joined forces with Jurgen and were now co-running the hotel with him. The aim was to turn it into an eco-lodge to welcome tourists – particularly groups of school children – and not only educate them about how to preserve the Arctic, but also to give them the tools to return home and be an activist for change. Maria was also going to take some part-time teaching at the school and Dad was going to help out on the science expeditions using his experience to help monitor the weather.

In the past few weeks, the four of them had redecorated the hotel foyer in bright colours to make it more of a welcoming place for guests and most importantly (as far as Dad was concerned anyway), he had shipped over his record player and entire Mozart collection. April had also finally persuaded Jurgen to relocate Hamish to his private quarters. Jurgen didn't mind. He was too excited because for the first time in ages, Svetlana was due to visit and apparently she couldn't wait to meet April. Even Granny Apples was planning a trip – and although she was grumbling about the temperatures, it did mean she was busy knitting lots of winter woollies to bring with her. Luckily, back home she had Chester to keep her company, who seemed more than content with his regular apple-pie dinners.

Life was certainly different this far north. When April wasn't at school or helping out at the hotel, she spent her free time with Hedda and the dogs. It was funny how they had become friends once they realised they were on the same side. Hedda had also changed her business.

Rather than taking tourists on sledding expeditions, she now focused on working with overseas corporate clients to fundraise for the protection of endangered animals.

And the best thing? Lisé had promised April that she could go on an expedition with her next summer! Although with some exceptions. Dad had been Very Insistent that April wasn't allowed to travel solo or try to cross any icy fjords. In the end she had told him about falling in and it had taken quite a few cups of strong tea to calm him down.

As April gazed out of the classroom window, she smiled softly. In the far distance, she could imagine Bear standing on his two hind legs, rearing up like a brilliant white stallion into the sky. If she cocked her head very slightly, she could just about hear the faintest rumbling of his roar. She was tempted to roar back, but suspected it wouldn't be the best idea. Not on day one anyway. Not that she thought the others would mind. They were all different here. As Hedda said, that's what the Arctic gave you – your true self.

'My name is April Wood,' she said, turning back to the teacher and smiling. 'But you can call me Bear Girl.'

The End

Author's Note

In 2019 I sat down to write a children's book. At that time, I was unagented, unpublished. But I knew, deep within my heart, that there was a story I wanted to tell. A story of friendship, of love, of hope – but most of all a story about making a difference.

That book would become *The Last Bear*.

When you write, you occasionally have a feeling that what you're creating is special. But I couldn't have foreseen just how intensely children (and grown-ups!) around the world would take Bear and April to their hearts. It's been so incredibly touching to witness.

And yet, at the same time, the most common refrain I heard was the need to find out what happened next. . .

How could you leave Bear and April separated like that? Will they *ever* see each other again?

The truth is, I always knew deep in my heart that I would revisit April and Bear's story one day. I couldn't just leave them. It has been such a joy to return and I hope you have loved April and Bear's reunion just as much as I enjoyed writing it.

As with *The Last Bear*, I must point out that befriending polar bears in the wild is never recommended! As cuddly as our Bear is, real bears in the wild are extremely dangerous, especially more so these days because of all the reasons mentioned in this book. So please do not approach a wild polar bear under any circumstances.

As always, any technical mistakes are purely of my own making. I am a children's author with a vivid imagination – not an expert husky sledder or an Arctic explorer.

In terms of the story, I had to take a few artistic liberties including distances covered and the location of some of the named places. The real Cole's Bay, for example, is in reality, right next door to Longyearbyen, but my version is larger and much more remotely located. Do check out a map of Svalbard (or there are even webcams!) to see the terrain for yourself. It really is one of the world's last wild frontiers and a place that takes your breath away.

It was important that in this book, April ended up living in Svalbard. This was always the end vision I had for her – that she would return home, not just to be with Bear, but to be at the very frontline of fighting climate change. Since the publication of *The Last Bear*, things have not improved – in fact in many places, including Svalbard, they have got worse.

In *Finding Bear*, Hedda points out some plaques which mark the spot where glaciers used to be. I took this idea from a tour guide I met on my research trip to Svalbard in which he mentioned this is indeed the case in certain parts of the world. It's frightening how quickly the world is changing under our feet in such a short space of time.

In fact, Svalbard is one of the areas most hit by climate change and is sometimes referred to as the fastest warming place on Earth. Experts from the Polar Institute are amongst those who calculate that Longyearbyen is estimated to be warming up at six times the global average.

The loss of sea ice impacts the polar bear's ability to hunt seals, so there are increasing reports of bears infringing upon human settlements in the desperate hunt for food. As mentioned in the book, this loss of ice also has a significant impact on mother bears and their young cubs. Since the 1980s, the amount of summer sea ice has halved and there are fears that by 2035, it will be gone altogether. The clock truly is ticking.

Unlike April though, we don't need to travel to Svalbard to save the polar bears. We can help in all the myriad of tiny, everyday actions that we each take to make our own backyard a healthier, greener place. Like I often say on my school and festival visits, small actions really DO make a difference. Imagine if every single person reading this book just did *one* thing. Wouldn't that be an amazing step to take – not just for the planet, but your own wellbeing too?

Since writing *The Last Bear* I have come to believe that true global change cannot be possible without massive government reform or big corporation change. It is not our children's responsibility to try to correct the mistakes of today. And yet, does this mean we do nothing? No. Because without grassroots activism and pressure on those who pass damaging climate policies, nothing will ever change. So, some of the things we can all do (especially the grown-ups reading this!) are sign petitions, write to our local MP, vote for MPs who support climate-friendly policies, look into how our pensions are funded and educate ourselves over the causes of climate change so we can start to make more informed life decisions.

Occasionally we *need* to make other people uncomfortable, or even make ourselves uncomfortable, to get things done.

April dreams of saving the world. When I was younger, I used to dream of becoming a bestselling author – but there was one problem. I was incredibly shy at school and hated speaking up in class. The thought of using my voice in public felt far too big and scary for someone like me.

These days I don't just dream of being a bestselling author. I realised it wasn't enough just to dream of *my* future. Now, I dream of doing my bit to look after the planet too. I hope my books shine a light on some of the most magnificent animals on Earth. I hope my books encourage other people to treat the world more kindly and most of all, I hope my books inspire others to follow their dreams too – especially if your dream is to make the world a better place.

The truth is, I don't think *any* dream is ever too big or scary. And if it is, all the more reason to go for it! Sometimes that's the only way we can create change – both on the inside and the outside.

There's one last thing to say and that's a HUGE roar of thanks. It's been an amazing journey so far and I couldn't have done any of this without you. But let's keep fighting. Let's keep mobilising. Let's keep roaring for a better tomorrow.

Love,
Hannah x

Resources and Further Reading

Here are some of the resources I used in my research that you might find interesting too:

Polar Bear International:

An international charity entirely committed to polar bears and their conservation. On their website, they have lots of educational resources, videos and articles.
www.polarbearsinternational.org

WWF:

A world of information about all endangered animals, including the polar bear and even how you can adopt one.
www.worldwildlife.org/species/polar-bear

Svalbard Webcam:

Can't get to Svalbard? Never fear. You can still check out this incredible place via six different webcams located in various different places in the archipelago.
www.webkams.com/svalbard-jan-mayen/svalbard

Polar Institute:

You can find more about their work in Svalbard here:
www.npolar.no/en/

A Simple Guide to Understanding Climate Change:

Climate change can be really difficult to get your head

around – even for adults. I love this clear and simple site from NASA which breaks down what climate change actually means and more importantly, how we can help!

www.climatekids.nasa.gov/kids-guide-to-climate-change/

Ecologi:

April decides to plant some trees to offset her travel to Svalbard by donating some of her pocket money. This is something I do too. I pay a monthly subscription and then donate more whenever I have to travel.

www.ecologi.com

My Website:

If you would like to stay in touch with me via my Bear Club newsletter or you just want to check out my Svalbard pictures, do take a peek at my website.

www.hannahgold.world

Whale and Dolphin Conservation Charity:

I am proud to say I am now an ambassador for this wonderful charity. You can find out more about their work here:

www.uk.whales.org

EXTRA READING:

Polar Bear Dens:
An article about polar bear dens in Svalbard and the impact of climate change upon polar bear populations.
www.npolar.no/en/newsarticle/where-do-polar-bears-den/

Thunder in the Arctic:
Thunderstorms in the Arctic are an incredible rarity, but with climate change they are an increasing phenomenon:
www.e360.yale.edu/digest/series-of-rare-arctic-thunderstorms-stuns-scientists

Svalbard News:
There's a weekly English language newspaper in Svalbard in case you fancy keeping up with the news over there!
www.icepeople.net

Books I Found Useful in My Research:
My World is Melting by Line Nagell Ylvsåker
A Woman in The Polar Night by Christiane Ritter
Spitsbergen – Svalbard: A Complete Guide Around the Arctic Archipelago by Rolf Strange

Acknowledgements

As always, writing a book is never a solo endeavour so thank you to everyone who has supported me along the way.

To my editor, Lucy Rogers for your kindness and passion for all things Bear. You worked so hard to turn around various edits before you went off to have your own little bear cub and for that, I am incredibly grateful. To Megan Reid for taking care of the final stages with such professionalism and who answers emails from me with endless patience, and finally, last but by no means least, to Nick Lake, who has overseen *everything* right from the beginning with such love and vision.

Massive gratitude to the *entire* team at HarperCollins *Children's Books* for making my publishing experience so AMAZING! To Cally Poplak, Alex Cowan, Laura Hutchison, Kirsty Bradbury, Val Brathwaite, Geraldine Stroud, Elorine Grant, Kate Clarke, Hannah Marshall, Carla Alonzi, Victoria Boodle, Jasmeet Fyfe, Jane Baldock, Aisling Beddy and Charlotte Crawford. And special thanks, as ever, to my wonderful publicist, Tina Mories.

Thank you also to Harriet Wilson and to Erica Sussman in the US.

To my agent, Claire Wilson, for encouraging me to trust my instincts and being there for me at all moments.

And to lovely Safae El-Ouahabi at RCW too.

Levi Pinfold – words are never enough, but thank you for making my books look so stunning inside and out. Bear would not have been Bear without you! Thanks also to Tamlyn Francis, Levi's agent.

Immeasurable thanks to Florentyna Martin for giving me one of THE greatest nights of my life when I won the Waterstones Children's Book Prize. And to all the Waterstones booksellers up and down the country who have embraced my books.

Gratitude also to Indie booksellers. You have been such cheerleaders of my writing from way back and you really are the beacons of the high street.

To all my publishers and readers overseas – you have shown me that stories of love and hope always transcend borders.

Thanks to all the festival organisers (here and abroad) who have invited me to spout on about bears and whales and drown out rooms with bear roars.

To Nicolette Jones and Alex O'Connell – both of whom picked *The Last Bear* as their *The Times* Book of the Week. Yay! And thanks also to Amanda Craig, Kitty Empire, Sarah Webb, Fiona Noble and Sally Morris for your championing of kidlit.

I don't think *The Last Bear* would have reached

half as many children were it not for the astonishing imagination and drive of primary school teachers. I am in constant awe of how you use my books in the classroom! A mega shout out to ALL of you. (Although a special thank you to Rich Simpson who donated a free *Matilda* theatre ticket to me!)

Thanks also to Books4Topics, Empathy Lab, BookTrust, ReadingZone, World Book Day and all the other hardworking people who make the children's book world such a magical space. Likewise, to all the tireless bloggers and tik-tokkers out there.

HUGE thanks to all the voters who picked *The Last Bear* as their winner for various book awards – including the Blue Peter Book Award, the Sheffield, Stockport, St Helens Book Awards and the Cowbell Award in Switzerland. I'm so happy you chose me!

To my author friends. I don't dare put any names because I know I'll miss someone out and then end up feeling guilty about it for months. But you're all so talented, kind, funny and generous. Big love to all.

As research for this book, I travelled to Svalbard. So special thanks to Tommy at Arctic Husky Travellers who answered countless husky questions from me and also to Natalie at Café Husky for being so welcoming.

Dr Huw Lewis-Jones – children's author AND real-life polar explorer – deserves credit for fact-checking my story. As does Alison Bond for reading a very early draft of this story but mostly just for being my best friend.

To my family for having to listen to me waffle on about polar bears for at least two more years. To my close friends and to my husband, Chris, who is my biggest support and has been with me since before Bear was even a glint in my eye. I love sharing this journey with you.

And finally, if you've made it to the end of these epic acknowledgements (I keep saying with my next book I'll try to make them shorter), it's to you – my readers.

The best part about being a children's author is not the reviews or the awards, lovely as they are, it's YOU. Your energy, your questions, your drawings, your letters, your enthusiasm, your bear roars but most of all, your desire to make the world a better, kinder place for humans *and* for animals.

This book was always going to be for you and I hope April and Bear's reunion has given you everything you wished for and more.